MILLENNIUM 3

RON FRAZER

Maryam Press
Bedford, Ohio

Millennium 3

by Ron Frazer

Second Edition

Copyright © 2018 by Ron Frazer

Published by Maryam Press, Bedford, Ohio

ISBN: 978-0-9600021-0-8

Buy additional copies of the book at:

http://www.ronfrazer.com

Acknowledgments

My friends Felora Ziari, Donna Amend, Linda Long, Dianne Bayless, and my wife, Sandy Frazer, have been so kind and helpful with comments and suggestions while reading the earlier drafts.

I am indebted to hundreds of people who have formed my vision of humanity's future, including the spiritual transformation currently in progress within individuals and the world community. I pray that as the third millennium unfolds, my vision is close to reality.

To Thich Nhat Hahn

who taught mindfulness to thousands

Preface

Five of my novels have been about women and their struggles. The idea for this novel began with some questions: what struggles would women have in a future world that was peaceful and had gender equality? What if education, health care and childcare were free? What if women were in primary control of governments, businesses and other social institutions?

I thought their struggles in the future would be more spiritual than physical. As the idea for the book started to solidify, I imagined three women, all around forty-five, who had losses that they were dealing with. Nadia is an artist who needs to make changes in her career. Mariha is the consummate mother whose children have grown. Huma is a widow.

If you would care to read more about the wonderful world these women live in before you enjoy their story, skip to page 147. The Epilogue contains many cultural details that are not in the story.

Thanks for reading,

Ron Frazer

November, 2018

Chapter 1

It is the fall of the year 2953 by the old European calendar. The year is 1109 by the calendar we use now. Our community is located in what was once called Virginia. Much has changed since then, but not everything.

« Mariha »

My name is Mariha Mutrib. At the moment I am stretched out on a chaise lounge on the balcony of my apartment on the 183rd floor. On my lap is a small computer screen, displaying the draft of an agreement for a client. I'm an attorney who can't seem to concentrate on such a warm, sunny day. My mind is wandering.

A communications window opens on my screen. I tap a button to answer the call. A smiling woman with gray hair appears in the window.

"Mariha, good afternoon."

"Good afternoon, Umma. How are you?"

"I'm having a great day, my dear. And you?"

"I'm sitting on my balcony, almost asleep."

She laughs. "Tell me: are you still interested in fostering a child?"

"Of course."

"Well, we have a young lady that needs a home for a while. She's fourteen."

Another window opens on my screen with an image of a pretty girl with black hair.

"Her parents are going through a rough time, and Samat — that's the girl's name — seems to be absorbing the stress."

"I'd love to have her stay with me."

"When could you come down to the council offices to meet with the family?"

"Anytime. Let me know what works for them."

After that call, I can't focus on the agreement even though it is due to my client tomorrow. Leaving it for later, I put the screen back in my briefcase, then close my eyes to check my feelings.

I'm excited about Samat coming to live with us. A fourteen-year-old girl should be an adventure. So there is excitement, but there is something else. I wish it were joy, but it's not. ... What is it? ... Something a little dark. ... A wave of melancholy washes over me. That's a shock. Where is that coming from? What could I possibly want to change in my life? If you asked me a few minutes ago, I would have said that my life was close to perfect.

I leave my eyes closed. After fifteen minutes, my mind clears.

Oh my God! ... Am I sad? ... I am, ... a little. ... Why? And this anger — what's that about? I have a loving partner, three sons all happily married, four grandchildren, a rewarding job, and great friends. Yet, here I sit, feeling that my life needs something more.

Without opening my eyes, I close my briefcase and set it beside me. After calming myself with some deep breaths, I search my memories for past happiness. Thoughts arise of my teen years with Nadia Fanan and Huma Nasik, my two best friends — how we were always giggling at some silliness. They were so much fun.

Nadia was always the artistic one. From our first day at school, she was making pictures that amazed the teachers. She could make things looks real while the rest of us were drawing stick figures. She had the heart of an artist, always looking for a way to do things differently from anyone else, whether it was her clothes or her choice of men. She married an eccentric musician named Radi. He is perfect for her — as creative in music as she is with graphics. The choices they make together amaze me. I never know what to expect from them. They must consider me boring. I always follow the crowd, but they never do. She didn't want to be average in any part of her life. She's one of the great artists of our pueblo with many of her images decorating public spaces.

Nadia and I got married the same year and had our children within the same five-year period. We spent endless hours together during the first ten years of our marriages, learning to be mothers, babysitting for each other, or sitting on a couch with our legs up if we could get the kids down for a nap at the same time. My son asked one day why he had two mothers instead of one like the rest of his friends. Once the five children were in school, we spent a little less time together.

Huma, my other best friend, was the spiritual one of the three. Even as a child, she was always looking for the noblest approach to every question. She was also the scientist. Nadia and I were not good at science, so Huma helped us through every science class. The three of us always did our homework together in one of the apartments.

Huma got married two years after Nadia and I. We both had one child by then, so she wanted to be a mother right away. After several months, they found that her partner, Jifah, was sterile. It was agony for her. Until our children got married, she was almost the third mother, spending many hours with them. She clearly enjoyed being Auntie Huma, but, for the first five or six years of her marriage, I would often see that her eyes were damp when she watched children playing.

Huma threw herself into her studies, then into her career as a compounding pharmacist. She and Jifah always were a warm couple who were pleasant to be with, but there was a tinge of sadness that surrounded them. I could see it in quiet moments if I looked straight into Huma's eyes.

So why am I sad? I still talk to Nadia and Huma every day. We giggle some, and could giggle more if we wanted.

When I let my mind drift, it is clear that my family doesn't need me as they did twenty years ago. Back then, there were the happy years of my twenties with my three little boys, one of them constantly clinging to the leg of my jumpsuit as I fixed a meal, or reaching up to me, so he could sit on my lap while I helped an older one with his homework. That feeling of being needed is missing now.

As my meditation continues, I see a longing for the silliness of the early years with my friends. Perhaps life has become a little too serious. The happy intensity of the relationship with my boys is also missing — boys who quickly grew to need me less and less. Lately, when I think of them, the thoughts are less about their current lives and more about their childhood.

It doesn't help to dwell on the past. Even though a part of me longs for the chaos of raising three boys or the laughter of teenaged girlfriends, I've got to find some new joys. Those joys are just out of reach; I can almost feel them. It is as if the answer lies behind a dense veil that reveals only the hazy outline of what I need.

* * *

A few days later, about 2 o'clock on a sunny, midweek day, I'm with Nadia. We're drinking tea at a wooden café table in one of the flower gardens near the south entrance of our pueblo.

We all live in the Whitetop Pueblo, a spherical structure almost 700 meters in diameter. The building stands on a slight rise above the valley floor. My partner, Amir, and I live on the 183rd floor, over 600 meters above the ground.

The spherical shape of the pueblo provides shade for extensive flower and herb gardens that surround the building — gardens whose meandering gravel walks are sprinkled with benches and small tables where people can enjoy the perfumed air and each other. During the warm months, the cool, fragrant air from the shaded gardens is vented up through the building for natural cooling. During the colder months, the warm air in the uppermost floors is pushed down to warm the building, then vented out into the gardens making them slightly warmer than the surrounding air.

Nadia and I are sitting in an alcove formed by low Azalea bushes. Both of us are wearing flowing jumpsuits of soft pastels, a typical outfit for women here, especially those whose bodies have developed Rubenesque proportions. We sit on wooden folding chairs, turned slightly toward the revolving doors of the lobby, so we can watch for Huma.

For people in our pueblo, or in any of the thousands of pueblos around the planet, the workday consists of three or four hours, either in the morning or the afternoon. The rest of the day is devoted to family and friends, hobbies or exercise. Years ago, Nadia, Huma and I decided to work in the mornings so we could spend a little time together each day.

We watch Huma exit the building, then stop to buy a cup of tea from old Mr. Ashai, a white-haired man with a wooden pushcart painted with flowers.

Huma is the tallest of us, and by far the slimmest, with beautiful, sculpted features. I have always loved watching her face as she talks. Her long, dark brown hair is frosted with gray and dances slightly as she walks toward us.

Nadia always describes herself as plain. Of course I see her as beautiful; I always have. She was slender as a girl, but, as she aged, her face took on softer, rounded features.

I am short, but a few centimeters taller than Nadia. My hair is long, straight and black. Even though the three of us are distant cousins, I must have received more Asian genes. My face is round with a small nose and epicanthic eyes.

As we watch Huma walking toward us, I quickly finish a funny story about one of my clients who bought one of the new levitation beds. The first time she and her husband tried to have sex, they bounced around between the force fields like balls on a pool table.

We smile as Huma sits down. She gives us a smile in return, but it seems a bit stiff.

"Is something wrong, dear?" I ask.

"No. I'm alright." She reaches across the table and strokes the back of my hand. "Some days, I'm a little sad

— just feeling alone. This is one of those days."

"I'm sorry, dear," says Nadia. "You and Jifah were married for so long — twenty-six years. ... Perhaps you're redefining yourself. You know — no longer half a couple — asking yourself, 'So who am I now?' Anyway, that's the way I'd probably feel if I suddenly lost Radi."

"Yeah, ... you're right; that's part of it. I don't know who I am. The last time I was single, I was eighteen. I'm no longer a girl, and I'm not a married woman ... only a grumpy pharmacist with too much time on her hands. I was thinking this morning that I don't seem like myself, ... whoever that is."

I'm still holding Huma's hand, lightly massaging her knuckles with my thumb. "What you are is a dear, dear friend."

Several laughing children rush past the alcove, momentarily reducing the volume of their ruckus out of respect for us older women. They burst with suppressed joy after running twenty meters farther down the curving gravel path.

I turn my head to stare at the children, struck by a memory from forty years ago, of the three of us as little girls, running and laughing down the same path. *I miss that silliness. I don't want to be a child, but do I want to be me?*

"I envy both of you," Huma says as she returns her teacup to its saucer. Her eyes remain fixed on the children whose laughter is fading to a tinkle as they disappear behind a curve in the bushes. "At least you have children and grandchildren to occupy your time. ..."

Huma continues talking, but I have stopped listening to her. I seem to be in a trance while staring at the point where the children disappeared.

Then I hear Nadia say, "How about you, Mariha?"

For a few seconds, I continue to stare into space, facing the last location of the children's laughter, now silent. "What?" I say, looking back and forth at my friends, embarrassed to be caught ignoring them. "I'm sorry; I was thinking about those children."

Nadia continues, "I was saying that I don't see my children and grandchildren often enough. They don't need me very much."

"Oh! ... Yes, ... same here." Then, after a long pause in the conversation during which each of us seems lost in her private thoughts, I say, "You know, I could use a change."

"What do you mean?" asks Nadia.

"I feel stuck in the past. For over twenty years, I defined myself as a mother. The children are still around, but I'm not their mother in the same sense — no longer caring for their needs throughout the day. I need to discover what it means to be a woman of forty-five, to find something new to generate some excitement or, at the very least, some enthusiasm." I look at Nadia, then at Huma. "Maybe you feel that way too. Right?"

Nadia returns my gaze, glances at Huma, then looks down at her empty teacup. She nods.

Huma closes her eyes and whispers, "You're right. I am stuck. ... Yes, ... something new. If someone asks who I am, only the words *widow* and *pharmacist* come to mind. That's not enough. I need a new word — a role with a little excitement."

I reach across and squeeze the hands of both my friends. "By tomorrow, I want each of us to have a plan for something new to get us out of this funk. ... Agreed?"

‹‹ Nadia ››

I'm standing on my balcony on the 172nd floor. It's an hour before sunset. My hands are gripping the stainless steel railing while I look at the surrounding farmland. I'm recalling the earlier conversation with my friends. The idea of being "stuck" bothers me. In the past, looking out at miles and miles of nature has been an inspiration. Maybe it will work today.

Stretching to the horizon in all directions, the peaceful verdure of the rolling hills seems to sing to me, like an a cappella choir of color. Concentric bands of various crops, comprised of every shade of green, surround the immense building that houses our community of nearly one hundred thousand people, both their homes and their businesses.

Radiating out from the sphere, are nine broad flagstone avenues that extend a hundred kilometers to reach the farms that feed and clothe our community. One of the avenues approaches the building directly below my apartment.

I notice some movement about two kilometers away. A speck is moving between the gray stripe of a recently harvested field and the dark green of some low crop, perhaps beans or kale. When the speck reaches the flagstone avenue, it turns toward the pueblo. The speck is too large to be a person. Perhaps it is a cart piled high with boxes of produce. Each afternoon, as part of the cycle of life at our pueblo, dozens of donkey carts bring fresh produce to the shops on the lower floors of the building.

After some minutes at the railing, I stretch out on a wooden chaise lounge. Now, the speck is clearly a cart approaching at the donkey's easy pace. Farther out, other carts appear. When the first cart is three hundred meters from the pueblo, I raise my binoculars for a closer look.

The farmer guiding the cart is a slender woman wearing khaki coveralls and a broad hat. She sits on the front edge of the cart, holding the reins loosely. I listen for the clop-clop of the donkey's hooves on the stones of the avenue, but can't hear anything over the buzz of the force field that surrounds the building, ten centimeters beyond the railing. The farmer and her cart disappear silently below the edge of the balcony.

I scan the fields with the binoculars. There are a few dozen farmers visible. Some are in the fields. Others are riding on one of several donkey carts, or walking home along the avenue. Since the fields extend for over a hundred kilometers, there may be a thousand more workers beyond the nearest hill, completing their chores before the imminent sunset. They will be loading themselves and the day's harvest into the elevated tube systems that connect the pueblo with the more distant fields.

I wonder how it would feel to make a living by growing food. Farmers are part of a natural process that continues relentlessly through days and nights, even after the farmer is home, washed, and enjoying her family. Would my evenings be more relaxed if I were a farmer? What if my work schedule tomorrow was completely out of my control, decided for me by the plants and the weather?

I am a forty-five-year-old artist, at present a rather unhappy artist, ten kilos overweight and short. I have been making illustrations and decorative art for thirty years. The job was enjoyable during my twenties — even into my thirties — but, for the last ten years, my images have been disappointing, merely modified copies of earlier work. I have run out of ideas. There are unwritten rules at this pueblo that force all art to be pretty and uplifting. I want to make art that shrieks my frustration, that claws at the boundaries of my world. Some days, I want to throw things.

My wonderful partner, Radi, is a musician who entertains in nightclubs on the weekends. He also works as a building mechanic during the mornings. Between us, we make enough money for our modest needs. We have two children, Shireen, a twenty-three-year-old girl, and Ramin, a twenty-one-year-old boy. Both are now married with small children. I love my family. They love me, but our relationships exist within some boundaries that seem to have become more constricted in recent years. When the children were young, every day was different. Now, each week seems like every other.

My eyes return to the western horizon where clouds have gathered. They obscure the farthest mountains and the setting sun. Nevertheless, the western sky is ablaze in a palette of oranges and reds. Overhead, the stars are coming out. My mind makes a connection between the splendid sunset and my work for the first twenty years, filled with a sense of creation and wonder. My recent images, like the overhead sky, seem to be slipping into darkness.

When did I become so ... morose? ... Could it be when Shireen and Ramin grew up, married and started their own families? ... Yes, ... Some of my happiness left with them. When they were small, I thought more about them than about art. There wasn't time for philosophy, for worrying about whether my images expressed my soul or whether they were merely a series of pretty pictures. After the children left, there was time to ruminate in this quiet apartment — maybe too much time.

I stand up, then return to the edge of the balcony. My hands grip the railing until the last purples in the western clouds disappear. Now dark gray clouds obscure the horizon. Above me is a clear night with a billion stars and a gibbous moon. They provide a faint glow over the landscape. The lightest bands of crops are still discernible.

I look down at my hands. They seem older — more wrinkles and a liver spot — a liver spot! — my first. It will be considered a big freckle for the time being. My knuckles are white. ... Where is this tension coming from?

I go inside, then into the kitchen to start slicing vegetables for our dinner.

I feel so guilty, worrying about a life that is ideal by any rational standard. I'm fed, housed, loved, and respected. If anyone knew about this unhappiness, they would probably laugh, saying something like, "I wish I had your problems!"

My thoughts wander to memories of my childhood. Why did I feel compelled to draw as a child? All children draw pictures, but my mother said I was obsessed with drawing. Was it for the applause? ... No. Mother and father barely acknowledged my new images: *That's very nice, dear.*

Was I dealing with some anger that was coming out through my art, even then? I remember being angry as a child. Not that there was anything to be angry about, it seemed to be a part of me.

Once Huma and Mariha came into my life, I felt happier. It was as if they were partners in my emotions. It wasn't true. They were actually happier than I was. Perhaps I used our friendship to rise above my anger, or to distract myself from it. For about ten years, we were engrossed in giggling about boys, other people we knew, and how our adult lives would be. I don't remember anger during those years.

Then we were all married. Mariha and I started having

children. We were so busy for the next ten years; there wasn't time to worry about anger.

Another ten years passed, during which our children got married and started their own families. I suddenly had hours of free time each day in which to sit, looking at images on my worktable, analyzing, searching for the inspiration that would generate the next image.

That was when the old emotions arose — that childhood anger that was never resolved during the thirty years that seemed a perfect life. I sat, and still sit, in an empty apartment, a silent apartment, feeling something that there are no words for. It is something that could be called anger, but maybe it is simply a craving or some deficiency in me. Whatever it is, it creates a silent pain that gnaws at my ability to concentrate.

Maybe it is a good thing. Maybe this — whatever it is — is there to push me toward a better me.

My mind wanders back to the conversation in the garden with Mariha and Huma. What would I change? If pushed toward a better me, who is she? What is the next step?

I know my art will change, but how? Perhaps the artist will have to change first, then the new art will follow from that. It's been said that people don't change. That can't be true. I'd hate to spend the rest of my life feeling the need to change, but not being able to do it.

Tomorrow Mariha and Huma will sit with me in the garden, sipping our tea. What will I tell them?

« Huma »

My long hair pulled back in a ponytail, I am cleaning out Jifah's closet. This is part of a larger project that includes going through the apartment, clearing out cupboards, bookshelves and closets of everything not needed for the next year or so.

It has been over a year since the aneurysm in Jifah's brain burst, leaving me a widow — sitting alone, stunned, hour after hour, trying, and failing, to put my life on a meaningful track. During the first several months, whenever attempting to imagine my future, my thoughts would be pulled into the past, into the pain of my sudden loss. That pain was a black hole, swallowing my hopes and energy.

Once able to resume working at the pharmacy, I enjoyed the distraction of my job. I didn't want to go home. Day after day, when my shift ended at noon, when it was time to return to the apartment for lunch, I found myself procrastinating by spending more time in the pharmacy or wandering the corridors of the pueblo, looking in the shop windows.

After my daily tea with Mariha and Nadia, there were long hours at home that found me taking too many naps, causing me to sleep poorly at night. Midnight would often find me wandering around the apartment or sitting in the dark living room, watching the sky through the window. Other times I turned on all the lights, then opened drawers and cabinets to examine the vestiges of twenty-six years of marriage. There was no joy found in the residue of my former life; it seemed to belong to someone else. It was as if I was in some other woman's apartment and looking at the mementos of her marriage.

The walls seemed to press in on me. During my marriage, I failed to notice how much the apartment had been defined by Jifah. I had loved him, had loved caring for him and creating a space where he could relax. But now, his continuing presence is overwhelming. I will save a few things — the photographs, and a few knick-knacks that we bought together. The clutter has to go — his clothes, tools, tennis gear, the things that make the small apartment seem more his than mine.

I'm standing in my kitchen, sipping some water. The closets have been cleaned out, and the liberated spaces dusted or vacuumed. There is a pile of junk gathered on the living room floor. A recycle shop will send some boys tomorrow to collect it.

I'm looking into the living room at the pile. I blow my nose, wash my hands, then slump on the sofa, exhausted, staring blankly at Jifah's belongings for a minute. With a groan, my chest falls sideways onto the couch. My head rests on the cushion. Only a few minutes pass before my neck and my side start to hurt. I stretch my legs out, then close my eyes. Some time passes; I don't know how much. My arms are cold, so I pull the blanket from the back of the sofa to cover myself. The cool trace of a tear trickles toward my ear. With the tips of my fingers, I wipe it away.

I open one eye to peer at the pile again. *This feels ... draconian. Why am I getting rid of all this? ... There's a nice racket; I could take up tennis. He always wanted me to play with him. Maybe Mariha would play with me. His clothes, yes, but some of his tools might be useful some day. Is this just an attempt to rip away the memories of him? ... If I put some of his things back, would it be denial? Would I be pretending that he has gone away for a few days, to return at any moment? ... Do I want that?*

No. ... I'm on my own. I need to become the kind of person who can be at peace when alone.

I close my eye, then dab at both eyes to clear the tears that are pooling in the corners. I visualize his empty closet as last seen: emptied, dusted and vacuumed. I remember standing there for some minutes, holding the handle of the vacuum, gazing through the open door at the worn wooden pole that had held his clothes, at the scuffed white paint near the floor on the right side where, over the years, he had tossed his boots.

Now, lying here on the sofa, — *Oh God! I'm crying again* — as I continue to visualize that barren closet, it seems to represent my recent life, empty and tired.

Perhaps the day after tomorrow, or the next, I will paint the walls of the closet a cheerful color, a pastel yellow, then varnish the woodwork. Holding the image of a freshly painted closet in my mind, I drift off to sleep.

* * *

Upon awakening, my mind is clear — well, as clear as it gets these days. The word "gratitude" drifts in. I start to list the things to be grateful for.

There were the twenty-six years with Jifah, but, in that thought, there is still too much grief for gratitude to squeeze in. I recall my forty years with Nadia and Mariha. Today, if forced to choose between my marriage and those friendships, I probably would choose my women friends. That wouldn't have been the choice twenty-seven years ago, but, at that time, I didn't know that choosing Jifah would mean having no children.

That was another grief that I have never gotten over. When we were young, Nadia and Mariha's five children were like my own in many ways, but, when I looked at them, it was with a mix of love and anguish. Since before they were born, I have loved each of their children and my love for them has grown each year, but they have been a reminder that I would never be a mother. Lately, while watching Nadia and Mariha with their grandchildren, I have the same mixed feelings.

I'm grateful for my career. The other compounding pharmacists and I make all the drugs required within the pueblo. It's a struggle to keep up with the evolving science of pharmaceuticals, reading the daily barrage of studies from around the world, and the recommendations coming from the planet's pharmacy council.

The level of work keeps my mind off my grief — mostly.

‹‹ Radi ››

I'm sitting at the dinner table, looking across at Nadia as we nibble on our salads. I can see that she is moody again.

"How did your work go today?" I ask.

She gives me an exhausted look, sighs, then says, "It was alright."

I know it wasn't. She had recently spoken about her frustration one night during pillow talk. As a musician, I understand creativity. I respect the artistic struggle for excellence. Nevertheless, her artistic quandary baffles me. A few weeks earlier, when she showed me the first few sketches that expressed this inner conflict of hers, I praised the composition and technique, but I couldn't relate to the message. It was as if I could see the notes and chords of her drawings, but not the phrases or melodies. I didn't, and still don't, know how to relate to an image that portrays psychological pain. In college, I saw angst in the ancient art from before the Calamity. In modern times, conflict in art isn't forbidden; it just isn't done. The conflict that existed throughout the world a thousand years ago is gone now. No one cares about it but the historians.

I wish I could understand her — understand what is troubling her at such a deep level. Whatever it is, can't she just set it aside and be happy. Our pueblo is peaceful and prosperous. Our children are thriving. We're healthy and so is the land around us. As I walk the corridors or the gardens, all I see are people enjoying their lives. Why get upset because people want artists to make pretty pictures?

I am studying Nadia's face as she looks at her bowl. I picture her sketches in my mind and wonder, *why bring the pain up? Does anyone want to see this?* Nadia's new pictures seem, at least to me, to be a needless rehashing of obsolete art. I know better than to tell her that.

Instead, I say, "I can tell something is bothering you. Please. What is it?"

"I met Mariha and Huma in the garden today. We were all saying we needed a change, or to change. You know I'm upset about my art. I don't know what to do. I know I can't sell the images I want to make."

"Can't you do both — make commercial images and the intense ones?"

Nadia gets up suddenly. She starts clearing the table. "No. Absolutely not! I cannot make happy, vapid pictures anymore."

I get up to help with the dishes. "So ... we're going to have to live on my income alone?"

"I'll find some way to make money." Her voice is a little loud.

"What would you do?"

Nadia grits her teeth. "Maybe I'll be a cook or a nanny." She spits the words at me.

"I'm sorry. ... I'm sure we'll be fine."

« Nadia »

The next weekend, I follow a boisterous young couple through the glass door of an art gallery on the fifth floor. Three of the long, white walls of the gallery are arranged with twenty-four, meter-wide, video screens in a single row. The new show represents work by three younger artists who went to school with my children. I scan the small crowd to see if Huma and Mariha are here. They aren't. I know almost everyone in the room;

the art community in the pueblo is small.

I wander through the room, greeting the other artists, glancing at the screens containing stills, holograms or short videos. When I feel myself starting to frown, I force my face to relax. The work is all so predictable. Every image is a variation of something seen many times before.

By the time I finish the circuit of the room, my agitation is probably visible. My hands massage my face, making sure the frown is smeared into a bland mask before anyone notices.

I decide to leave, but as I turn toward the door, Huma and Mariha walk in. They are laughing at something one of them said. They smile and wave, but my returned smile is tight and insufficient to hide my mood.

"What's wrong?" whispers Mariha as she puts her arm around my shoulders.

I look around to make sure none of the artists are close enough to hear. "This stuff is boring and repetitive. Every image is only a pretty picture, a slight variation of something that's been done a dozen times. I'm sorry. I'm so tired of this trend."

Mariha slips her hand into the crook of my arm. "They all look nice to me, but walk us around and show us what you mean."

The three of us stand in front of the nearest screen which is showing a short, dreamy video of nature scenes overlaid with pastel mists that slowly change color. I pause while looking for the right words. After watching the film for a few seconds, I whisper to Mariha and Huma, "There's nothing wrong with this work, but there is already a screen in the bank lobby showing a film very much like this, and two more in restaurants. You've seen them, right? ... We need something new."

"They *are* a bit boring, aren't they?" says a voice behind us.

I gasp. The three of us turn to face a younger woman who, judging by the flowery, cotton kaftan she is wearing, is obviously from another pueblo.

She holds out her hand to me, "I'm Latifeh."

I take her hand and continue holding it while saying, "I'm sorry; I hope you're not the artist. ..."

Latifeh smiles. "No. ... No, I'm from Fairy Stone Pueblo — just visiting friends for a few weeks."

"Have we met before?" I ask, tilting my head a little while studying her face. "You look a little ... familiar."

"I believe we have — a few years ago. You had some new pieces on display in one of the lobbies."

"Now I remember. You complimented the work ... even though my images were similar to these."

Latifeh smiles, but blushes. "Well ... the art in my pueblo tends to be less about scenery."

"These are my friends, Huma and Mariha."

Everyone shakes hands. The four of us tour the remainder of the exhibit while Latifeh and I become deeply involved in a whispered discussion of the theory and history of art.

After the last image is dissected, we all go to a small café on the same floor for tea. The room, which holds about fifty people, is nearly full. There is an infectious and joyous mood, a din of happy voices. Working our way to the back, we find a booth bounded by two worn wooden benches with high backs. Latifeh and I sit together on one bench. Huma and Mariha sit on the other. The server takes our order for a pot of tea, then Latifeh and I continue our enthusiastic comparison of trends in modern art.

"Do you have any photos of work from your pueblo?" I ask.

"Yes, quite a few." Latifeh pulls out a screen, then quickly flips through images until she finds the ones she is looking for.

Turning the screen so the four of us can see it, she begins to slowly page through dozens of their current work. "As you can see, our art is not as soft as those by your people. We prefer images that are crisp and lifelike but stir the imagination. We often find a fragment of a scene that speaks to us rather than including the entire vista. Here are two good examples: a few autumn leaves." She slides another image in place. "... and a closeup of some rocks in a stream."

The slide show goes on for some minutes while Mariha and Huma sip their teas. I'm afraid they are getting bored. When Mariha finishes her tea, I notice her squeezing Huma's hand. Huma nods.

"Those are very nice," says Mariha, sliding out of the bench, "but we're going to leave you ladies to chat."

"I'm sorry if we got carried away," says Latifeh as she and I stand up to hug them.

"Not at all. It was interesting meeting you," says Huma.

Huma and Mariha leave, working their way through the café, greeting several friends on their way out. Latifeh and I sit down, then resume flipping through the photos.

"I'm excited about these images," I tell her. "They are pretty, but that's not the point they're making. ... They force you to look beyond the beauty, don't they? — to appreciate what the artist is saying."

"Exactly. There's a message in each image, ... but it's

subtle and open to the viewer's interpretation."

She hands me the screen so I can look at my own pace while she finishes her tea. I spend ten minutes looking through the images, getting more excited, making embarrassingly loud sounds of surprise or pleasure at several of them. When I see that Latifeh has finished her tea, I hand the screen to her.

"Before you return to Fairy Stone, come visit me," I say, transmitting contact information from my screen to hers.

"I would love that," she says, glancing down at the incoming message. She slips the screen into a large, tapestry shoulder bag.

As we pass through the crowd on our way to the door, I introduce Latifeh to several people from the art community. We ride the elevator up to the residential floors. When the elevator stops on the 136th floor, Latifeh holds the doors open, then turns to me, "Are you free tomorrow?"

* * *

The next afternoon, Latifeh is at my studio. We are sitting at my worktable, flipping through my recent images as they float on the rear of the angled, glass surface, about two meters wide and a meter deep.

"I've never seen such, such ... These are very strong images," says Latifeh. "... such intensity of feeling!"

"I *am* experiencing something intense. Although, the feeling isn't exactly clear. I'm exploring my emotions through this series. Here's the most recent; it resonates with me more than the others."

I stretch the image to fill the worktable. We pick up our teacups, then roll our chairs back a little to study it.

"You're the first artist I've met who is doing this kind of work. It would be great fun for you to come visit Fairy Stone. You should meet our people to talk about what you are doing. It would give you a chance to see their most recent work and hear them explain it themselves."

"Oh, I don't think so."

"Why not?"

"I've never been away from Radi. For that matter, I've never left the pueblo."

"Why not?"

"All my family is here. My work is here. I enjoy seeing films of other places but have never felt compelled to visit them. We're so comfortable here. "

"Wow! ... Well, do you feel compelled now?"

"Hmm ...," I smile. "Maybe I do."

« Huma »

The following afternoon, Nadia and Mariha are sitting on the sofa in my living room, sipping tea and commenting on the new furniture arrangement. The room is much less cluttered. I eliminated a large, tattered chair that Jifah used and some chests where he stored his tools and sports gear.

"I like it," I call from the kitchen while arranging a few buns on a plate, "but, it doesn't feel like my home yet. It was the old way for so many years."

"Give yourself some time," says Mariha, "it will grow on you."

"You get so much sun since you're on the south side of the pueblo," says Nadia, "some plants would do very well by your windows."

I smile while settling into the chair opposite them. "Yes, that's a good idea. ... The other day we talked about making changes. Clearing out the apartment is only my first step. The next step hasn't made itself known to me yet, but it'll find me at the right time."

Nadia says, "I've been considering some changes too. Latifeh invited me to come stay with her at Fairy Stone for a while. Maybe that's my first step."

"You can't!" gasps Mariha.

I look at her, surprised.

She continues, "What would Radi say?"

Nadia says, "He'll be shocked. He may not agree at first, but he'll get over it."

I tell her, "I think it's a great idea. We're all in such a rut. We need to shake things up a bit."

"But, ... what about us?" says Mariha. "We always have tea in the afternoons. I'll miss you."

"When I come back, we'll have much more to talk about."

Mariha isn't crying, but her eyes are red and moist. She gets up, then stands at the windows to look at the fields. After a minute, she turns around to face Nadia and me, then says, "Since we were five years old, we've never been apart. You are both more than sisters to me, more than friends. I can't imagine not seeing you every day."

"I promise it'll be a quick trip — maybe a week or two at the most."

I walk over to Mariha, then rub her shoulders. "I'll miss Nadia too."

Tears start falling down Mariha's cheeks. "I'm sorry. ... I've been trying to imagine changes, but keep coming back to the friendship we've had for our whole lives, to how we've supported each other through our marriages and motherhood. I'm so afraid that any changes will affect our relationship."

I look at Nadia, who is still sitting on the couch. She is looking back and forth from my face to Mariha's.

Nadia puts her teacup down, then stands to join us in a group hug. She says, "You are both a part of me, an essential, wonderful part of my past and my future. I have to make this trip. I promise it won't change our relationship, at least not in a bad way. We each want to make changes in our lives. Right? That means to stop doing things that are boring while finding new exciting things to replace them. It would be crazy to stop doing the fun things we've shared for the last forty years. My art is boring. That's all I want to change. Really! That's all! With a new direction in my art, I'll be happier and have a stronger relationship with each of you. "

While we continue our hug, I kiss their cheeks, then say, "You're right, Nadia, it's the right thing to do. We can't make progress if we keep doing the same old things. Change is always a little uncomfortable, but in the end, either we arrive at a happier place, or we learn a lesson about a change to avoid. Either way is progress."

Chapter 2

On a sunny morning a few days later, I'm in a capsule flying through the elevated tube to Fairy Stone Pueblo at several hundred kilometers per hour. During the fifteen-minute trip, badly blurred scenery, mostly green, streaks by.

As the capsule slows, I see Latifeh waiting for me on the platform. With a whisper, the door slides open. Latifeh and I greet each other, then walk down a ramp to the flagstone avenue that leads to her pueblo.

I have my first clear look at a pueblo that is completely different from my own. It appears to be an immense pyramid with the top cut off about half way up. The base is perhaps two kilometers on a side, the height a half kilometer. Latifeh points out that each layer of the sloping sides is formed by the patios of the apartments on that floor. Almost all the patios have enough flowers and plants hanging over the walls to make the pueblo appear more like a meadow-covered hill rather than a manmade structure. I love the natural feel of this pueblo.

The walk to the pueblo is half a kilometer, so Latifeh puts my bag on one of the donkey carts that carry people and freight to and from the tube. As we walk along behind the cart, I can see that the basic layout of the surrounding farmland is similar to my own: concentric rings of various crops, tubes and broad, flagstone avenues radiating out to serve the carts that take the farm workers to the fields and return with their daily bounty. Along the way, we pass an old man in coveralls with a smaller cart. He is scooping up piles of manure for use in the fields and gardens. All seems similar to Whitetop except the shape of the building.

We take the elevator to the seventeenth level. The corridor is straight and very long; I can hardly see the end of it. At Whitetop, the corridors curve with the building, so there is never a sense of great distance.

Her apartment is on one of the four inner slopes of the pueblo. She sets my bag in the guest room, then walks to the wall that separates her apartment from its patio. There is a rectangular doorway, about three by four meters, which is protected by a force field. She switches off the field, so I can explore the patio. I cross to the far wall, which is about a meter high, and look around at a manmade structure that is unlike anything I've ever seen.

The four inner slopes of the pueblo begin at the ridge that rings the pyramid and terminate at the edges of a square park. The inner slopes are much like the outer slopes with foliage cascading from the walls of each patio. Unlike those on the outer slopes, the inner residents lack the view of the surrounding fields and distant mountains. Still, the natural beauty is striking.

As we stand at the edge of her patio, Latifeh tells me the inner park is one square kilometer. I see trees, ponds, soccer fields and playgrounds, all connected with gravel paths. Hundreds of people are scattered throughout, enjoying the warm sunny day.

A gentle breeze murmurs in the greenery of the nearby patios. I hear a bumblebee buzzing. Occasionally, the high-pitched shriek of a joyous child transcends the distance. At Whitetop, there are never natural sounds inside the building. The gentle hum of the mechanical systems is the usual sound. On our small balconies, there is always the buzz of the force field that shields us from the weather.

"You don't have a force field protecting you!" I say, a little surprised.

"No. We need the rain for all the plants."

"Oh! ... I hope it rains while I'm here. I've never felt any rain. Sometimes it rains when I'm in our gardens, but the building shields us."

"I'll make us some tea."

"Thank you."

I walk around the patio, admiring the plants and peeking over the short walls into the patios to the right, left and below. Each has its own selection of flowers and vegetables. At Whitetop, it isn't practical to grow much on the balconies.

"I invited some people over for tonight," says Latifeh, as she rejoins me with a tray of tea and cookies.

"Artists?"

"Yes, all of them. I told them to bring some of their latest work to share. It should be fun."

«« Mariha »»

Huma and I are sitting at our usual table in the garden beneath Whitetop. The old man with the painted push-cart moves down the path, having left us with fresh cups of hot tea and raspberry-filled pastries.

I say, "It seems so strange with Nadia gone. It's disorienting."

"I know. When Jifah died, it was similar — the feeling that someone is missing, someone who has never been missing."

"There's no comparison to what you went through, but, with Nadia gone, even though it's only for a few days, there is a grief. I don't relish change, even though we talked about the need to make changes. I'm very conflicted."

"None of us like change, but we said we needed it, didn't we? ... Perhaps we should all be traveling more."

"What do you mean?"

"Well, ... isn't it amazing that none of us have left Whitetop in forty-five years?"

After a long pause, I say, "I simply never thought about leaving. ... I never had any desire to go anywhere else."

"Yes, but was that because you were busy with your family?"

"I don't think so. ... Everything was here: my family, friends and work. There are pictures of all the other places. For me, that's enough."

Huma seemed to be thinking for a few seconds. "But now you could take a vacation if you wanted — go to the sea in the tube and wiggle your toes in the sand. It's only two hours to get down there."

I considered a trip for a moment, but it scared me. "Being by myself wouldn't be a vacation; it would be torture. ... Maybe we should go together."

"In my opinion, you should go by yourself. It would be

more of an adventure."

"I don't want an adventure! I want ... I want to laugh the way we did when we were girls."

"I agree we haven't been laughing much lately," says Huma. "We *should* find something to laugh about. We could all use more happiness, but what I want more is joy."

"What's the difference?"

"Perhaps joy is a more mature form, involving love and contentment. The other day, when we saw those laughing girls in the garden, it gave me joy. I looked at their happiness with the wisdom that an extra forty years allows me. I imagined their next twenty years when they'll find romance and have their babies. So maybe joy is happiness mixed with wisdom."

"I can be joyful here at home."

"Yes, but if you go somewhere for a few weeks, you'll look at your life differently when you come home."

"Would you go somewhere by yourself?" I asked.

"I've never thought about it. ... Hmm ..."

"See, you're afraid to do it!"

"No, I'm not. ... I'm going to do it. I'll go to the beach for a week; then, I'll come back and tell you about my adventures. Maybe I'll have some misadventures that we can laugh about. Then, you'll have the courage to go."

"I was teasing you. Please don't go. At least wait until Nadia comes back."

« Nadia »

Latifeh's guests begin arriving at eight o'clock. After the last group shows up, everyone moves out onto the patio where Latifeh has set up a home theater. A dozen, mismatched chairs face a large video panel. On a table are drinks and snacks.

Each artist takes their turn, pulling a small screen from a satchel or purse and transmitting several images to the panel. There is universal appreciation of the artwork – polite oohs and aahs, even occasional applause. I enjoy the show, am fascinated by almost every image, but perceive patterns and similarities among them.

I had asked Latifeh to put me at the end of the evening. I show my first image, a simple one of a couple dancing. There is silence for a moment. People lean forward in their chairs. Someone says, "Hmm."

I put up another image.

"It's similar to Tamara de Lempicka's work," says a woman in a bright blue kaftan. "No one has done work like hers for hundreds of years."

"Yes, — but more like Edward Povey," says a man after he walks up to the screen for a closer look. "de Lempicka was more relaxed. Povey was intense, as in this image.

"Povey was one of my favorites," I tell them. "When I first saw his work, I felt as if his paintings came from a part of me."

I show several more images, each one more intense than the last. There are a few gasps. The final images show disturbing relationships between people. Some of my audience are squirming.

I say, "I know my images are quite different from yours. They are different from anyone else at Whitetop. I am a bit troubled lately. These images come from that troubled place."

There is an embarrassed silence.

Latifeh stands up and offers, "I thought it would be

interesting to bring Nadia here so we could discuss this type of art. We're all happy with what we're doing, but I don't see any strong emotions in our art — any of it. I see some questions in our images, some answers, but not emotions."

A man who had shown work that was very geometric and abstract says, "We got away from using images of people some time ago — many years ago, in fact. I believe we have all decided that using people emphasizes the personality too much."

"Yes, but is that valid," asks Latifeh. "At one time, most art showed people. It was used to force humanity to look at itself, to examine its beauty and its warts."

"We all have warts," says a woman with a particularly sour look on her face, "but I find it tasteless to portray them in art."

"Possibly," says Latifeh, "but I think it's an interesting question. If you look at Nadia's images as abstractions, as colors and shapes, they are beautiful. It's only when you see them as real people and start questioning what's going on in their heads, or in their relationships with each other, that they become disturbing."

I ask the group, "Here at Fairy Stone, do you have a rule that art can't be disturbing?"

"Well, ... no ..."

"That seems to be one of our rules at Whitetop," I say. "Somehow we have narrowed our standards so that art can only be pretty, never disturbing in any way. Let me show you this other collection, some of my earlier work plus pieces by other Whitetop artists."

I project about fifty images, each for only a second or two, every one a soft-focus, pastoral scene of lakes, mountains, or fields with people working.

When the last few dozen are projecting, I slow down, leaving them on the screen a little longer. As the artists view the last two or three, I say, "You see what I mean, very pretty but very repetitive, no emotion, no personal statement, no insight into the human condition, no idea what was going on in the artist's mind."

A man who had been quiet up to now says, "Well, I agree with you about those images, but I can't see myself making images like your recent work. I want to make people think, but I don't want to show them what's in my mind, and I don't want to use people in my art. I consider it vulgar."

Latifeh steps forward to defend me. "I'm sure all of us have strong opinions about what works for us, and what our clients want to see. Can we get together again in a few days to discuss this after we've all had a chance to process what we've seen? I'll contact you soon."

The group nods their agreement, then shifts into chit-chat mode. They eat the remaining snacks, finish the two pots of tea, then, by twos and threes, they leave.

"How do you feel?" asks Latifeh as she starts clearing the snack table.

I begin collecting glasses from around the patio. "I was surprised. In the work you showed me, there was clearly an underlying meaning, so I thought some of the artists here might be working in a more emotional style. It was a shock that people would interpret the portrayal of people as vulgar."

"You and I both realize that the artists in your pueblo are in a rut," says Latifeh, "but so are we, only in a different rut. It's good to have standards in some things, but art needs to evolve. Are we going to be making these same images in a hundred years? In a thousand? There needs to be someone who is ahead of the crowd — far enough that the work forces us to consider what we want, but not so far that we can't relate to the work. You've shaken us up a little. We won't do what you are doing, but I'm sure we'll change our standards."

I stand at the counter while Latifeh loads the dishwasher. "Did you ever wonder how these standards get created?" I ask her. "Did someone a hundred years ago have a meeting where they decided that your artists would make sharp, bright abstracts and our artists would make soft landscapes? Or was there an artist who was so loved that other artists imitated her style, which then became a standard without anyone discussing it?"

‹‹ Mariha ››

I am walking with Huma through the vegetable market on the second floor, our baskets on our arms.

"Mariha, dear," says Huma, "I'm leaving for the Gulf Coast the day after tomorrow."

I stop, feeling my eyes brim with tears as I look at her then down at the pepper in my hand. The tears run down my cheeks.

With my voice cracking, I say, "With Nadia gone, I was hoping we could spend more time together, not less. ... You can't go. It scares me for both of you to be away at the same time."

Huma moves closer to me, then puts an arm around my shoulders. She is so tall; her head rests on top of mine. I feel her long hair against the side of my face.

She says, "I will miss you too. I truly will. But I need to be alone. I love you and Nadia, but right now — just for now — you are both something of a distraction."

Horrified, I jump back from her. I set my basket down, then look through my bag for a handkerchief.

Huma puts her arm around my shoulders again, then

kisses my cheek. She says, "I love you. I could spend several hours a day with you, and it would be fun, but it would be keeping me from considering who I am and what my next step should be."

"Maybe what you should be doing is spending time with me," I look up into her face, then smile at her, weakly.

Huma smiles back, hugging my shoulders tighter. "That's possible. We'll see when I get back. ... I feel as if I'm surrounded by people so much that I can't decide what's best. My life is always about what others need. I only need to take a step back, not run away."

"I understand that you need time alone, but if I don't see you ...," I choke. I have to wait until the lump in my throat allows me to continue, "The three of us have seen each other every day for the last forty years. You are as much a part of who I am as Amir or the children."

"As you are a part of me," says Huma, "but I don't under-stand why this trip is so threatening to you."

"You said before we're in a rut. ... We are, but each of us may be in a different rut. You're feeling a need to pull away, but I'm feeling a need to grow closer. It seems my life is full of people that love me, but they aren't very close — the way we were close thirty years ago, the way my family was before my sons grew up and left. I want to laugh, and I want to feel needed. There isn't much laughter in my life lately, and all my relationships feel superficial — even with my family, you and Nadia. This pulling away that you're proposing makes it feel even worse."

"I don't want to hurt you, my dear," says Huma. "We'll keep in touch while I'm away. Look for a message from me with pictures every day. Whatever changes occur for you or me, they won't affect my love for you. I'm sure Nadia feels the same."

I tell her, "This morning, I was reading a quote by Albert Schweitzer, *If you love something so much, let it go. If it comes back it was meant to be; if it doesn't it never was.* That sounds true, but I'm still frightened."

« Nadia »

Latifeh and I are having breakfast on the patio the morning after the second party with the artists. The previous night's discussion wandered wildly in many directions. It eventually settled around the idea that they all needed to explore their artistic boundaries — that maybe they had become a little too comfortable and had devolved into mutual admiration without honest criticism.

I am spreading jam on a piece of toast while Latifeh is commenting on the need for honest critics in any artistic community. My screen pings. There is a message to call Hazar, my mother. I use my screen to dial home.

"Mother, I had a message to call you."

My mother is crying. She stumbles through some unintelligible words. After a few seconds of silence, another voice comes on the line, "Sweetheart, it's Radi. I'm so sorry. Thabit died this morning. They don't know why yet."

"Oh! ... Not Daddy! ... No. ... He wasn't sick!"

"Your mother said he was normal when they went to bed last night, but this morning he was gone. He apparently died quietly in his sleep."

"I'll, ..." I'm struggling to get my constricted throat to work, "I'll come back on the next tube," I whisper. "I'll call you back."

Latifeh tells me the tube is leaving in an hour. She helps me pack; then, we walk to the tube terminal. A digital display shows the tube will arrive in three minutes. We sit on a bench holding hands. I am crying softly.

"Is there anything I can do for you?" asks Latifeh.

"No. It's the shock, you know. I was very close to my parents. They were both wonderful. Daddy was a tailor. He made all my clothes. This jumpsuit is one of his. I was always so proud of my wardrobe. It felt as if I was wearing his love for me."

"That's a lovely metaphor — to be surrounded by his love."

As we sit waiting, I send a message to Radi, Huma and Mariha with my arrival time.

"I'll come to Whitetop for the funeral," says Latifeh. "Please, let me know when you have the details."

The tube arrives with the sound of a thousand people sighing. The doors hiss open. We hug. I squeeze her hands, then nod my silent goodbye. My voice isn't working at the moment.

* * *

Huma, Mariha and Radi meet me at the terminal just before noon. The day is cool but clear.

As we begin walking to the pueblo, I ask, "How is Mom?"

"I spent the morning with her," says Radi. "She is in a daze. It's such a shock to everyone. As you know, your Dad was never ill. The news was posted on all the screens this morning. Half the pueblo seems to be calling to offer their condolences. ... The funeral will be tomorrow afternoon. "

"What about washing the body?"

"Two of the other tailors and I will wash and wrap the body later today. The coffin makers will have the coffin finished tomorrow morning. Everything is arranged."

We enter the lobby of the pueblo. As we step into the elevator, I say, "I'll go straight to Mom. Radi, please take my bag home, then join me."

When Huma, Mariha and I reach mother's small apartment, the door is open. Hushed voices are spilling out into the corridor. I stand at the edge of the living room, which is full of people. Neighbors and friends of my parents are wandering in and out to pay their respects. There is little room to move.

Mother is standing in a far corner with my uncle Amin, my brother Tali, and my son Ramin, greeting the stream of visitors that, no doubt, has been flowing in all morning, bringing hugs, kisses and dishes of food. I push my way gently through the crowd to give Mother a long hug. As I kiss her cheek and look into her moist eyes, I know there is nothing to be said at the moment. I enter the kitchen to help with the food.

My daughter, Shireen, and Mona, Ramin's partner, are already cooking in the small kitchen. They are preparing a large pot of stew. Loaves of fresh bread are piled on the counter beside several casseroles. I take one of mother's aprons from a drawer, tie it on, then begin cutting up a chicken for the stew.

I see Mariha and Huma slipping through the crowd toward the door. They wave to me and make a motion with their hands that they are leaving. They know I'll call if I need something. Nothing needs to be said.

As I handle the body of the chicken, pulling the muscles away from the bones, then slicing the meat into chunks, I visualize my father's body on the porcelain slab down in the coffin maker's shop, how yesterday it was a seemingly healthy body doing everything that bodies do; then, in a moment a few hours ago, it became only a body, as lifeless as this chicken, only meat and bones.

I believe in the life of the spirit, that my father is here in the same way his spirit has always been here, but no longer connected to a body. My physical life with him is over. Tears erupt down my cheeks again.

I never considered a day when he would no longer make my jumpsuits. In my mind, I would forever be able to walk up behind him at his sewing machine, put my arms around his neck, smell the oil he used on his hair and feel the scratchy stubble on his cheek. That had been my habit since I was a tiny girl, tall enough to reach his neck as he sat on his stool.

Tears slip down my cheeks. I look forward to the end of this day, so I can sit by mother, hold her hand, and feel the presence of the love between my parents without the noise of all these people. Mother's tired face appears for a moment in the gaps between the people that surround her. She raises a handkerchief in her left hand, then dabs at her reddened eyes as each well-wisher moves away and another takes their place.

I know my mother is getting tired. I'm glad the crowd is starting to thin out. Soon, it will be only the close family; then we can all eat together.

* * *

It's seven o'clock. The food has been eaten and the leftovers have been put away. My children and grand-children left to return to their apartments. My grand-parents, Mother, my brother and I are able to sit to say some prayers for Father. We include prayers for tests and for gratitude that he shared our lives for a while.

Mother asks me to spend the night. She doesn't want to be completely alone yet.

* * *

The next afternoon, the service is held in a chapel on the 191st floor. Afterward, the crowd goes down the elevators to follow the horse-drawn funeral cart to the cemetery, about a kilometer north of the pueblo on the top of a rounded hill. At the grave site, the simple wooden coffin is carried by six pall-bearers. They place it in a larger granite coffin that is waiting inside the grave. The granite top, engraved with Father's name and lifespan, is lowered into place. A glass headstone with a nine-pointed star above his name will be added later.

My brother chants the prayer for the dead while a hundred friends and family stand with heads bowed. The cemetery workers close the grave as the group follows the empty funeral cart back to the pueblo. On the way, we pass another funeral procession that is on its way to the cemetery. My brother whispers that the coffin maker told him they average three funerals each day.

* * *

I stay with my mother for the next week, helping with the details that need to be addressed. This was the first time that either of us had experienced a death of someone close to us.

Two days after the funeral, she and I visit the registrar of the pueblo to sign some papers that record the death and put the apartment in my mother's name. We drop by the bank and other offices to ensure that their records have been updated.

That evening, as mother and I are talking after dinner, the medical examiner arrived to deliver a copy of the death certificate. He explains that Father died of a virus in his heart that interrupted the electrical signals. So his heart had simply stopped beating sometime during the night. He expresses his condolences, then leaves.

I've always been so proud of Mother. She and the other wellness doctors keep the people of the pueblo healthy. They do such a thorough job that chronic illnesses are rare. While there are surgeons who repair the occasional injury or genetic mistake, for the most part, doctors like mother spend their days advising patients on their lifestyles and consulting with the pueblo management on ways to ensure that the ecology surrounding the pueblo remains healthy so that every living thing thrives. They work with everyone from soil scientists and water treatment engineers to the people who devise the school lunches.

She tells me that she will take the next week off. The other doctors can easily handle her responsibilities.

« Huma »

It is late afternoon, a few days after the funeral. I'm expecting Nadia and Mariha for tea. On my way home from the pharmacy, I stopped into a flower shop to pick up three bouquets of flowers to brighten our moods. Yesterday, I bought two new jumpsuits, a little brighter than normal for a middle-aged pharmacist. I'm wearing the yellow one. It is the most cheerful outfit in my closet.

Nadia and Mariha arrive together at four. I lead them into the dining room where the table is set with tea, pastries and a bouquet of yellow carnations in a crystal vase.

"How is your mother doing?" I ask, pouring the tea. "Would she want me to drop by to chat, you know, widow to widow. Of course maybe it's too early."

"Yes, too early," says Nadia. "She wants to be alone with her feelings. She doesn't seem to want to talk much. I don't mind though. The suddenness of it — I can't stop thinking about it. The images keep reappearing. We should have had another thirty years with him. He seemed so healthy."

"I felt the same way when Jifah died. There was no warning at all. He simply went to work one day and collapsed. We were supposed to grow old together."

"It frightens me," says Mariha as she reaches for a bagel. "My day is centered around Amir now that the kids are grown. What if he popped out of my life the way Jifah and Thabit did?"

"For myself," I tell them, "if I can be whole and happy when alone, then I can enjoy another person without fear. I don't want a man in my life for a while, but when I do, no one will be needed to complete me. Someday, once the grief has passed, someone can share my joy, not make me happy."

"I don't know how to do that," says Mariha, her fore-head wrinkled.

I tell her, "Neither do I, but the answer is out there somewhere. I'm taking the tube to the Pensacola Pueblo tomorrow."

Nadia says, "Oh! ... I didn't know you were going anywhere."

Mariha rolls her eyes. "Yes. She's running away from home!"

"For how long?"

"I'll be back in a week. Perhaps being by the ocean will give me a chance to think. It's great that you're back early. Now you can keep Mariha company. She was concerned about us both being away at the same time."

Chapter 3

« Huma »

The capsule arrives at the Pensacola tube terminal mid-morning. The weather is perfect, clear and much warmer than at home. I walk to the pueblo, which is a glass and metal sphere almost identical to Whitetop. It stands a few miles from the Gulf of Mexico in the low hills above the site of the old town, which has long since disappeared and been covered over with agriculture.

After dropping my bag in a rented apartment, I go to a café in the pueblo to eat a saltwater fish I've never heard of — a treat since we only eat freshwater fish at home.

I'm anxious to see the water, so, with some other tourists, I ride a cart down to the beach. On the way, we pass a replica of part of the old town that was founded thirteen hundred years ago by the Spanish. Some of the tourists get off to visit the site, but I will save that for another day. After rumbling another half kilometer, the cart stops at a visitor's center near the beach. It's a wooden pavilion with toilets and maps of the area. The other tourists walk to the beach with their blankets and umbrellas.

As I examine a large map on the wall, a park ranger walks over to ask if there are any questions. The short, round woman reminds me a little of Nadia.

"I want to walk along the beach. I'm not looking for anything in particular."

"Before you leave, if you're interested in the history of the area, there's a display to your right. There were European Americans here for five hundred years, until the flooding during The Calamity. Before the Europeans came, Native Americans were here for at least a thousand years. Well, ... I'll leave you to explore."

The map indicates that the beach extends for miles east and west. I pause at the edge of the pavilion to admire the beautiful sand, as white as sugar. The water is clear and peaceful, turquoise near the beach, then progressively darker shades of blue as the depth increases.

Stepping onto the sand, I find it pleasantly warm, so I remove my sandals. The fine texture of the sand surprises me; it's almost like flour. The sun is very hot on my pale skin, so I open the large umbrella left by my kind landlord with a note stating that a wise visitor would take it along to the beach.

Turning to the west, I walk along the edge of the Gulf with the cool water sloshing over my feet. After a kilometer or so, a subconscious feeling makes me stop. Looking at the southern horizon over the glistening water, I take a step forward, so the water covers my feet. The feeling is gradually becoming a thought: I am standing at the junction of the land, the sea and the air. For the first time in my life, there is a realization that there is only one body of seawater on the planet since all the oceans are connected. There is only one land mass since the land is all connected under the water. And, of course, there is only one sky. Any names — Atlantic, Pacific, Africa, Asia — are arbitrary, for our convenience.

Standing there alone, I see myself as the tiniest speck at the junction of those three greatest parts of the Earth. I am an atom. My insignificance startles me.

As I continue to the west, tiny plovers, barely larger than sparrows but with long legs and beaks, are running at the edge of the water three or four meters ahead of me. They stab their slender beaks into the sand to eat miniature white crabs or shellfish. To my right are eroded chunks of concrete that jut above the scrubby saw palmetto plants. The concrete is all that is left of the homes that once filled the beaches of western Florida, as it was known hundreds of years ago. Before long, these last vestiges will be dissolved, becoming part of the beach sand.

Continuing westward, the beach turns to the north into a small cove. Across the water is an old woman sitting on a blanket. She raises her hand in greeting. I wave back. For the next twenty minutes, I walk around the cove, then approach the woman who turns to me when we are close enough to speak. She is very old, perhaps a hundred years.

"Welcome," she says. "I was hoping for some company. Why don't you sit down to rest a while?"

Without waiting for an answer, the woman scoots over to allow me room to sit on the blanket, facing the water. We are in the shade of some tall slash pines, so I close my umbrella, laying it beside me as I sit down.

"My name is Huma. I'm here visiting from the Whitetop Pueblo."

"I'm Tamala. I come here most days to meditate. Would you care to join me?"

"Yes, I started meditating a few months ago, but have never tried it outdoors. This will be a new experience."

"For myself, I focus on the sparkles on the water. You do

whatever you prefer."

I smile, then close my eyes. I use a mantra to meditate, but soon open my eyes to enjoy the water while the mantra continues in my mind. There are no sounds other than the hissing of the water as it caresses the sand and the whisper of wind in the pines. There is a profound peace. The thought wanders through my mind that some of this peace may be coming from Tamala.

About the time that my legs become stiff, Tamala stirs slightly. The old woman stretches her back by leaning forward, resting her upper body on her thighs as she reaches to hold her feet. I lower my gaze from the silver horizon to a crab, scurrying around the edge of the water. It is the size of a small coin, white, almost translucent. After a minute or so, I look over at my new friend.

"Thank you for allowing me to join you."

"Thank you for coming to join me." Tamala smiles. "Have you found what you were looking for?"

"Am I looking for something?"

"Judging by your age, I assume you aren't here to have fun splashing in the water. You're looking for an answer."

I smile at her insight. "You're right. My partner died a year ago. Now I'm trying to decide who I am. I was telling my friends that the last time I was single, I was a young girl. I don't know how to be single at my age."

"Do you want to be married? That would be a simple solution."

"That doesn't feel right. Even if tempted to marry again, I would still need to redefine myself first."

She smiles. "True. Your meditations will eventually lead you to the answer. Give it time. Don't rush. ... But, here's a thought ..."

"Yes."

"When you were married before, you were exactly who you are now, but there was an illusion that you were different because you were married. Now that illusion is gone, but you're still looking at yourself through the lens of a married woman. Life is asking you to drop your illusions. Whoever you truly are — she is perfect for this moment in time."

I was awestruck. It felt as if God was speaking to me through her. "Can you say that again, please."

"The woman you truly are, right now, is perfect for where you are on your path, but you must look at yourself honestly and not through some distorted lens — a lens formed by the ideas of someone else."

"Thank you, Tamala. That feels right. ... Perhaps I should be getting back. ... Would you like to join me for a meal this evening? It would be my treat."

‹‹ Mariha ››

Nadia has had tea with me each afternoon since Huma left — in the gardens if the weather is warm enough, or in my apartment. Today we are sitting at my kitchen table.

I am pouring us a second cup of tea. "You remember, a few weeks ago, when the council contacted me about Samat, the girl whose parents had asked for someone else to take her for a while? The council told me that she's ready to come live with us."

Nadia raises her eyebrows. "And you're going to do that?"

"Yes, it'll be like having a daughter. She's fourteen and has been deaf since birth."

"Why haven't they corrected her hearing?"

"They tried. It seems to be something in the sound processing areas of the brain that can't be repaired."

"Are you sure you're ready to take on a teenaged girl?" asked Nadia.

I smile. "It'll be an adventure, but I should be able to give her what she needs."

"I'm excited for you."

"I don't know what it is like to live with a deaf person."

"I don't either. ... Why do her parents need someone to take her?" asks Nadia.

"I'm told there's some unhappiness between them that needs to be resolved. Samat seems to be absorbing the family stress. They're concerned about her."

"When is this going to happen?"

"Tomorrow. ... I can't wait."

« Huma »

At sunset that evening, I walk into a seafood restaurant on the 197th floor of the pueblo. Tamala is already there and smiles when she sees me.

Before sitting down, the view from over six hundred meters above the Gulf captures my attention and draws me to stand by the window in awe. The curvature of the Earth is quite visible in the silvery arc at the horizon. Below the silver is the deep blue of the gulf, which fades, as it approaches the shore, into lighter and lighter shades of turquoise until it ends at the meandering white line of the beach. It might be the most beautiful sight of my life.

Tamala has chosen a table next to the window. I kiss her on the cheek, then sit down across from her. She smiles, then pats the back of my hand as it lies on the table.

"It might be worth it to move here," I tell her, "so I can look at this view from time to time."

"It is marvelous, isn't it?"

The server arrives, takes our orders, then leaves.

"Tell me a little about your life, Tamala," I ask. "What did you do for a living? You must have a large family."

"I was a farmer until I was eighty-one. I loved my few hectares of dirt. I grew flowers mostly. Some vegetables too."

"And your family?"

"I had four children; three of them are still alive. There are fourteen grands and ... I don't know how many great-grands and great-greats. You lose track of them, don't you?" She laughs. "They are all here in the pueblo."

"What of your partner?"

"The first one died early; he was sixty-nine. We were married for fifty-three years. He was the father of my children. I married twice later on. Number two lasted ten years. Number three only six years."

"Are you going to marry again?"

Tamala smiles. "No. You can't train these old men as well as you can the young ones. If I could find a thirty-year-old interested in an old girl like me, it might be worth another go." She laughs again. "I won't hold my breath."

I have to laugh. Her eyes twinkle, then she starts laughing even louder. The servers look over at us. She looks around at their concerned faces, then covers her mouth in mock embarrassment.

We both look out the window for a few minutes, then I ask, "Would it be too much to ask how you were after your first partner died? How did you get past your grief?"

"I don't mind talking about it, dear. It was a long time ago. You mentioned today about the difficulty of deciding who you are now that you aren't married. I'll start with that."

"Thank you."

"I can tell you that when the second and third partners died, it was much easier. Who I was after they died was the same as before we were married. But after my first partner died, — we were both sixteen when we married — I was a different person at sixty-nine than I was at sixteen, so I couldn't simply slip back into my old life. I suppose I went through what you're going through now."

She pauses for quite a while as she looks out the window. I begin to wonder if she's lost her train of thought.

"I can't tell you what I did," she continues, "but I went back to my farm after a few weeks. I visited my children as always. After a year or so, I had an enjoyable life again. There wasn't anything specific that turned some grief switch off inside me."

"How many years passed before you married partner number two?"

"It was ... four years — no, five."

"So you married him after the grief had passed, somewhat?"

"That's right. You know, sometimes, even today, a memory will float through my mind, bringing out a tear or two. The grief doesn't leave you completely. It does become ... sweet. It's bitter at first, but later it becomes sweet."

She smiles. So do I.

While we are smiling at each other, the server brings our meals.

"What do you think turns the memories sweet?" I ask as we begin eating.

She looks at me for several seconds, then looks out the window for a few minutes. She says, "Time passes, I suppose. Memories fade or change. What's left, at least for me, is a sense that something good happened for fifty-three years. The pain of his death isn't there anymore. The memory of that pain is there, but I can't feel the intensity of it."

We finish the meal with small talk. I pay the bill. We walk to the elevators. As she gets off on her floor, we hug. The doors close.

* * *

It's almost midnight. Not able to sleep, I stand at the window in my nightgown, looking out at the Gulf. The water is agitated. The moon is reflecting in the waves, turning almost the entire surface of the Gulf to silver. For several minutes, I stand there, watching the glistening water. Maybe this is a meditation, maybe not. After some time, my legs start to hurt. Sleep may be possible. I get back into bed, take some deep breaths and wait.

The dream starts with Tamala and me on the blanket,

looking at the sea as we were today. She is sitting on my right side. I feel someone sitting next to me on the left. I know who it is.

I'm sitting with my legs crossed, my hands in my lap. He puts a hand on my knee. I look down at his hand, but am afraid to look at his face. I don't know why.

"Is it good — where you are now?" I ask.

"Everything is perfect. There isn't place or time, but somehow you're with me often. Whenever you think of me, we're together. I try to send you love; sometimes it seems that you feel it."

"I miss you."

"I know. There is a wisdom in this separation. Remember it will only last a few thousand days. After that, our reunion will last forever, thousands of centuries and thousands again."

"I loved you so much," I say. "I didn't realize how much."

"There will be an eternity to love again. During these few days of separation, learn the lessons that life gives you. Remember that there is no separation for me, only for you. You are already with me."

His last sentence repeats until it becomes a mantra: *You are already with me. ... You are already with me. ...*

Some minutes pass. I realize that his hand is gone, so I look to my left. There is no one there.

I look to my right. Tamala smiles at me.

‹‹ Mariha ››

It is early afternoon. I'm cleaning up after lunch. Amir has just left to help a friend paint his apartment. Samat is at the kitchen table with her computer screen, doing her homework. She moved in with us a few days ago.

"Miss Mariha," says Samat in her usual loud monotone, "are you happy that I'm here?"

I turn to the small computer screen that I keep connected to her screen. I open a voice-actuated chat window, so my speech appears on her screen.

```
Mariha:    At this moment, I can't imagine
           anything that could make me
           happier. This is the first time
           I've had a girl living with me.
           You are a treat!
```

Samat smiles. "I don't think my parents were glad that I was with them."

```
Mariha:    They may be unhappy at the moment,
           but not with you — perhaps with
           each other. Soon they will be
           happy again. It will get better.
```

"They've been unhappy for a long time."

```
Mariha:    You're welcome here for as long as
           you want to stay.
```

Samat stands beside me, then puts her arm around my waist. She looks down at my screen as I speak.

```
Mariha:    Dear, I want you to help out a
           little. I need you to do the lunch
           and dinner dishes, but I'll do the
           breakfast ones because you have
           to get to school. And straighten
           your bedroom before you leave in
           the mornings. Can you do that,
           please?"
```

Samat walks back to the table, then sits down. "Mother never made me do stuff like that," she pouts with her arms folded in front of her.

```
Mariha:    When my children were small, I
```

```
                 didn't ask them to do housework
                 either. You're getting big enough
                 that you can help.
```

Samat looks up at me. The pout is still there.

```
Mariha:      This is your last year as a child.
             You're becoming a woman. It's an
             important time for you. Give some
             thought about what it means to be
             a woman. I'm here if you want to
             talk about it.
```

« Nadia »

I'm walking along one of the avenues about a kilometer from the pueblo. I've been doing this the last few afternoons since Mariha is getting to know Samat, and Huma is finding herself, or, at least, trying to find herself.

I love Mariha and Huma, but spending some time alone is good for me. In ninety minutes, I can walk about three kilometers out, then turn around and walk back. I'm losing some weight and feeling better.

From up close, the colors of the crops are so different. From my balcony, it all looks green, but close up there are so many colors, from the yellows of the peppers to the purples of the eggplants.

My mind returns to my art. The colors around me are barely noticed as I struggle to find some new direction. The pretty pictures of the past — they'll stay in the past. The last few were tinged with sadness. They were still pretty, but I could see my mood in the color choices.

What am I going to do?

I have always been an artist. I remember the thrill as a little girl with my first screen, when the end of my finger brushed over the glass, leaving a trace of color behind. There has to be some way to satisfy my drive to create something new, to produce art that is useful to the community.

I turn around to walk back. The sun is reflecting in the glass of the pueblo. It's too bright to look at, so I walk with my head down slightly, the brim of my floppy hat shading my eyes. After a kilometer or so, I notice that I've been in a daze, not noticing any of the fields passed, nor remembering any of my thoughts.

I reach the gardens that surround the pueblo, then walk a little down the path to where we often sit, hoping to see Mariha or Huma. They aren't there. I head for the entrance. When I enter the foyer, some neighbors wave to me. I wave back. While waiting for the elevator, I look back through the glass doors at the avenue. I don't have even a hint of a solution to my artistic quandary. I take the elevator to the second floor, then walk the circular hallway past various shops and businesses, examining the art that is displayed along the hallway or in the shop windows. Most of the art is on video screens, but there are a few sculptures and tapestries. Nothing appeals to me.

I take the elevator up another floor, then begin walking that corridor. I'm frustrated with myself for being stuck in two dimensions. I enjoy seeing sculptures, ceramics and tapestries, but can't see myself doing those commercially. I'm exhausted as my art survey of the third floor is completed. Having seen nothing that gives me any ideas, I take the elevator up to my home.

A chai in hand, I sit at my worktable. A tap on the screen wakes it up. Another tap opens the communications function and a third selects Huma. A window opens showing it is connecting to Huma's screen.

"Hello, Nadia," says Huma. The video is blank.

"Hi, do you have time to talk?"

"I can call you a little later. Is that alright?"

"Thanks. Call me when you've got a few minutes."

"I'll call this evening."

I touch the terminate button, then call Mariha. There is no answer, so I call Latifeh.

"Nadia! I'm so glad you called! I've been thinking about you."

"I've been thinking about you, too. Do you have time to talk for a while?"

"Yes, I do. What's up?"

"I'm considering giving up art as a profession. As you know, I'm very unhappy with my older work. I certainly can't make any money with my mid-life crisis series. Other art forms like sculpture, writing or music don't seem right. I feel as if I'm in the bottom of a deep pit. Everywhere I turn there's a steep climb with no clarity about where it might lead."

"Do you have other skills?"

"Not really. I've always worked in two-dimensional art."

"Wow, ... you know, I'm the same way. ... I've been thinking about you, about how unhappy you've been making commercial images. The only idea I had is to make videos — not decorative videos, but educational stuff. At least some of your skills would transfer, and you might enjoy working on a team."

"Thanks. I hadn't thought of educational materials. I'll go down to the job bank here. There may be someone looking for my skills."

After some chit-chat about the artists at Fairy Stone, we say our goodbyes.

* * *

The next day, I am speaking to Maryam Habibi, a smiling, white-haired woman at the pueblo's administrative office. She keeps track of who needs work and who needs workers. We sit on either side of a glass-top desk on which the current database is displayed.

"Right now we're at almost full employment," says Maryam. "There are maybe a dozen people looking for work. There are only these few businesses that are hoping to hire someone."

She rotates the window around, so I can see the job openings. I stare at her desktop.

Hmm ... A few shops need workers. ... That could be fun. ... I'd get to meet more people. ... But it doesn't feel quite right. There are farms that need help with the harvest. Why does that attract me? ... Maybe I need a radical change.

"I don't know what I want to do," I tell Maryam.

"I'll send you this list, so you can decide." Maryam taps her screen a few times. "Let's keep in touch."

I take my screen out of my bag to check that the list has arrived, smile at Maryam, then put the screen away. We stand to shake hands. She says she will let me know if any art-related jobs become available.

* * *

Back in my apartment, I unlatch the door to the balcony to stand at the railing, contemplating the farms and the workers. The day is cloudy. A half meter in front of my face, rain drops are bouncing off the force field like diamonds on a sheet of glass.

Do I want to be out there in the rain harvesting crops? ... Well, ... they need people. It's only for the season.

The next day I call Maryam Habibi to tell her I want to help with the harvest. Maryam tells me that I can start the next week, and who to contact for more information.

* * *

That night, I call Mehreen, a friendly woman who owns a cabbage farm. Mehreen tells me where and when to join the other workers, and what to wear. She knows I've never done farm work before. There's a hint of laughter in her voice.

I have three days to prepare myself. Since the last thirty years have been spent sitting at a desk, growing plump and soft, I vow to spend the next few days limbering up and reading everything available on harvesting cabbage.

Chapter 4

« Mariha »

Nadia, Huma and I have been unable to meet regularly for a few weeks. I decide to call them. It is evening, almost too late. I tap my screen to start a three-way video call. Within seconds, both their smiling faces are on my screen.

"I miss you both," I tell them.

They concur.

"Anything new to report about your new family member?" asks Nadia.

"I'm enjoying my time with Samat," I tell them, "but she is trying my patience. I never had a daughter before, only sons. She's just being a teen on the one hand, and, on the other, expressing the anger she has absorbed from her parents. There's a boyfriend who I haven't met yet. She is being willful about seeing him more often than I would prefer."

Nadia says, "Why don't I come down some evening. I can spend some time with you and Samat. Shirin was the same way at that age. Some of my experience may be useful. What do you think?"

Huma is sipping a tea in her little window on my screen. She puts her cup down, then says, "I would help, but I don't remember being that age — other than the fun the three of us had together. I remember being quite happy. Maybe Samat needs a few girlfriends."

I look at my image in the video window on the screen; I'm smiling. "I haven't heard her talk about girlfriends. It might help if she had some. Nadia, can you come down tomorrow evening, so we can chat with Samat?"

"Sure. Call me when you and Samat are ready."

"Huma, how are you doing?" I ask.

"Well, I told you about the old woman in Pensacola. I've been meditating about everything she said to me. It seems that this grief is going to take a few years and can't be rushed. I was in too much of a hurry for the grief to end. Tamala taught me that the pain will only be worse if it is given energy by my attempts to push it away."

"Ooh, that sounds so wise. What else did she say?" I ask.

"She said the grief process was a little like taking a long walk to somewhere you very much want to go. You can flog yourself at each step because you haven't reached the end, or you can enjoy each step, being content with your rate of progress. She used the analogy to explain that as we take each step forward, we have to give up the previous location of our feet. So, if we want to rise to some new spiritual level, we have to relinquish who we were a moment ago. It's like death-birth, death-birth, over and over."

"Wow!" Nadia says. "I'm tingling. ... That analogy could help me as I search for a new direction in my art."

"You're still struggling with that?" I ask.

"Yes, … and I'm no closer to an answer. Maybe my process isn't unlike Huma's grief. It could take some time to change."

Huma says, "I had a dream about Jifah while in Pensacola."

"I'm tingling again," says Nadia.

"He told me he's with me whenever I think of him."

"That's wonderful," I say.

"He said that, for him, we aren't separated at all. Only I can feel the separation."

"I've read that the dead are more aware of us than we are of ourselves," I say. "It's nice to remember that our ancestors are aware of us and perhaps guiding us."

‹‹ Nadia ››

The morning is chilly. A mist moves among the rows of crops on either side of the avenue. I'm sitting with four other women on the back edge of a rumbling donkey cart. I'm on one corner; two are sitting in the center; and the other two are at the other back corner. Mehreen is in front holding the reins. The wooden wheels of the cart make a syncopated rhythm as they thunk across the gaps between the flagstones. The sphere of the pueblo grows smaller as we make our way to the cabbage field.

The other field workers are talking and laughing. I try to find a conversation to focus on, but, to me, the four voices and the racket caused by the cart combine, making it hard to follow either conversation.

Mehreen calls out, "I'm sorry girls. Hold your breath; Henry must have been eating romaine lettuce again."

My companions are all burying their faces in their jackets. A cloud of flatulence from the donkey passes.

Once the air clears, we all break out laughing.

I should make more of an effort to be friends with these women. They're all pleasant. During these few days that we've worked together, they've shared upbeat, intelligent conversations. Why haven't I joined it? Maybe I've been an artist for so long that I've become an artistic snob.

I scoot a little closer to the two women in the center, so I can hear them better. They are talking about the slippery elm tea that one of them is taking for a sore throat. Both women notice that I have moved closer, smile, then pause for me to say something.

I tell them, "My mother is Dr. Khayat. I've often heard her suggest that herb for sore throats."

The woman smiles. "Yes, she recommended it to me. She's my doctor. Tell her it seems to be helping."

"I will," I say, smiling back.

The two women continue talking, but now include me through eye contact. It's a first step.

Something flitted through my mind, something about art. I try to get it back, but can't. It was a brief thought, something about seeing reality.

« Huma »

It's evening. I'm meditating on the couch in my living room. The incense burning on the coffee table is producing a sweet, jasmine scent, but a little too much smoke; it is annoying. I can only take shallow breaths; if my inhale is too deep, the smoke catches in my throat. Should I stop the meditation to move the incense into the kitchen? No, I can deal with it. Tomorrow, the incense will be farther away.

Shallow breath in with cool air, out with warm air. In, out, ... in, out.

After twenty minutes, my timer goes off with a soft chime. I sit with my eyes closed, no longer meditating, just thinking. A description of dharma in a recently read book starts me thinking.

I can consider dharma as my role in the orderly flow of the universe. The book suggested a river as a good analogy. When floating in the center of the current, resisting attachment to anything seen along the banks, I am in tune with the flow of the universe. The strong current carries me along swiftly and effortlessly.

If I become attracted to something on the bank, if I try to remain still in the water, then I have to fight the current. This takes great effort and is not in harmony with the universe. Trying to go back in time by swimming upstream, takes even more energy.

I remember Jifah's laugh, then feel a tug — my heart yearning for my old life. Allowing myself to live in the past requires swimming upstream. Staying stuck in today's grief is analogous to fighting the current, trying to stand still. To be in harmony with the universe, I have to move with the current, but where is it? How does one choose actions that are harmonious? I have no idea. Is non-action an option? ... No, I can't do that either.

Imagining the river of dharma makes me feel peaceful, but it doesn't tell me what to do. Of all possible thoughts and actions, which of them is in the main current of the river? Find a boyfriend? Change jobs? Move to Pensacola? ... Stay as I am?

‹‹ Mariha ››

Nadia comes to visit after we finish dinner. I made a rhubarb pie for dessert. Amir takes his pie into the living room to watch something on the screen. We three girls sit around the kitchen table with our computer screens and our dessert plates. We all open a chat window.

I'm nervous. The right words aren't coming to me. I don't want Samat to feel we're meddling or controlling her. I'm grateful when Nadia opens the conversation.

Nadia: Samat, how is school going for you?

"It's alright."

Nadia: When my daughter was your age, she went through a short period where all she and her friends thought about was boys.

"I don't hang out with the girls who are boy crazy. I find it boring. I don't hang out with the other girls either. None of them seem to like me much."

Nadia: Why is that?

"I'm the only deaf student. Maybe it's because I'm different, or maybe they can tell that I don't like them either."

Nadia: When I was your age, I had Mariha as my friend. I loved her so much, and I still do. It only takes one girl to make you feel loved and accepted. The others don't matter so much. Is there one girl who you could be closer to?

Samat thinks as she slowly chews a bite of pie. "Maybe there is one girl."

Nadia: Has she been a little nicer to you than the others?

"Yeah, a little."

Nadia: And you've got a boyfriend. Tell me about him.

"His name is Wertah. He's very serious — wants to be a doctor."

Nadia: How old is he?

"He's fifteen but seems older."

Nadia: He sounds like someone I might
           pick for you if you asked my
           advice.

"Well, you could meet him. Mariha doesn't like him."

Mariha: I do too! He seems very polite.
           But, I'm nervous about boys.
           I don't want someone taking
           advantage of you. Sometimes
           when we're unhappy, we make bad
           decisions.

"I have to make my own decisions. I've almost reached the age of maturity."

Nadia: True, you will be fifteen next
           year, but even women as old as
           me can make bad decisions. It's
           good to talk to people who love
           you before making an important
           decision.

"So, do you love me, Mariha?"

Mariha: I know you want me to be honest.
           I am learning to love you. We've
           only been together for a few days.
           If you are here long enough, I'm
           sure I will love you like my own
           daughter.

"I'm not going back to my parents. I want to stay with you until next year; then, I want to marry Wertah."

A gasp escapes me. I look at Nadia for help. Samat is

looking at the screen, so she doesn't notice the shock on my face.

Nadia: Have you discussed marriage with him?

"No, but he has talked about his future as a doctor, and that he hopes I'll be part of his future."

Mariha: Samat, I believe we should spend more time with Wertah. I've only met him twice and for just a few minutes. Don't you agree, Nadia?

Nadia: Yes, I do. Samat, we're only concerned with your happiness. There is no other agenda. Can you ask Wertah to come here to meet us?

"I don't think he would want to meet both of you."

Nadia: You're right. I don't need to meet him. Next year, if you decide to marry, you know you'll have to have permission from Wertah's parents and from your parents. They might ask for the opinion of Mariha and Amir before they say yes. I think Wertah should begin to develop a relationship with your parents and with Mariha and Amir.

"Do you already have a bad opinion of him, Mariha?"

Mariha: No, not at all. As I said, he seems nice. Honestly, Samat, I respect your judgment. You are a very serious young woman. I suspect he is a very nice person, so I won't have any problem with

```
               him. Let's see what happens as I
               get to know him better.
```

```
Nadia:         Who are Wertah's parents? I wonder
               if we know them.
```

"His father is Farash Dakan. He owns a bedding shop on the third floor. His mother is Zafaf Dakan. She works in a shop that sells women's clothes."

```
Nadia:         I know Farash. A few weeks ago we
               bought one of the new levitation
               beds from him. He was very
               pleasant to do business with. I
               don't know Zafaf, but my father
               probably knew her.
```

"They have both been kind to me. I like them both."

The three of us continue chatting for another hour about Samat's life and our families. The conversation grows more relaxed and friendly. Samat initiates a hug with Nadia as she leaves us.

‹‹ Nadia ››

It is early morning. The air is quite crisp. The donkey cart turns from the avenue onto a gravel path. We're traveling between a field of soybeans and another of corn. There are workers harvesting both crops. The cart makes a constant crunching sound as it rolls over the gravel.

The pueblo is in the far distance. It looks like a child's marble, a glimmer of sunlight bouncing off its surface. The thought strikes me that all my art, all my life's work, is inside that little glass ball. There's a brief thought, something about art. Before my mind can grasp it, the thought fades.

We reach the edge of the cabbage field. I hop down, then face Mehreen, who is standing on the cart next to a pile of large baskets. She tosses one to each of us.

As I walk to the beginning of the two rows that will be my morning's work, I examine the basket. It is truly beautiful; a design is woven into the sides using different colors of straw and reeds. It surprises me that someone would take the time to decorate such a utilitarian object. The design woven into the basket seems to clarify the hazy thought that slipped away earlier: this farm work, at least for the moment, seems more real than the images I had produced at my worktable.

Yes! That was the earlier fleeting thought: the cabbages in my hand are more real than images projected on a screen in a restaurant. Today I am one of a thousand workers who are out this cold morning, gathering the food that will keep the pueblo alive for a few days. The thought makes me feel more vital. If this work is left undone, there are consequences. If one of my pretty pictures were left unmade, what would be a tragedy?

This is something of a revelation. I don't know what it means for my career.

« Huma »

Having finished my evening meditation, I'm lying on my back on the couch, contemplating the thoughts that drifted through my mind like falling leaves. I love these rare moments of clarity. It seems as if the meditation calms me, so troubling thoughts can be set aside. During this afterglow, this moment is revealed in its inherent simplicity, less clouded by my fears.

I visualize myself walking on a long spiritual journey. One step at a time. My current location, this step, is perfect. There isn't a need to go back to before Jifah died. Neither is there a yearning to rush to a later time when my grief will have mostly dissipated. I'm fine here — now. This is the right place for me, the right time.

These words ring true, but they don't describe what is going on in this grieving heart — not completely. On some level, it is still sad, longing for the life of two years ago. On a higher level, this heart knows that it is as it should be at this moment. Maybe tomorrow or the next day, it will take another step. The woman living in my body at that point will be perfect for that stage of her journey.

Chapter 5

« Nadia »

Today is the last day of the harvest. We are riding the cart along the avenue, heading back to the pueblo with baskets full of cabbages. Mehreen is in front, holding the reins. The rest of us are in the back with our legs dangling over the edge.

We're tired, but there is a joyful mood among our little crew. Maybe we're glad our work is finished for the year. There will be no work in the fields until the spring planting.

I've made friends with Farah, a slender woman about my age, but she looks much older. She has always been a field worker, so her face is leathery and deeply lined. I've never known a happier person. I love watching her face as she talks. She has smiled so often over the years that when she relaxes her face, there is still a bit of a smile in the lines around her mouth. Her happiness is contagious.

After we arrive at the pueblo, we unload the baskets of cabbages, then gather around Mehreen to receive her thanks and hugs. As we all walk to the elevators, I grab

Farah's hand. "Would you care to come for tea after we've cleaned up?"

Farah arrives at my apartment an hour later. This is the first time I've seen her in casual clothes, a flowered jumpsuit and canvas flats. In the fields, she always wears a broad-brimmed hat that hides most of her hair. Now, it is brushed and just touching her shoulders. It is a lustrous gray.

I invite her into the kitchen where a pot of tea is ready. After we are seated and the tea is poured, I ask, "What are you going to do through the winter months?"

"Each winter I assist in the school with the younger children. There are some that need a little extra help with reading practice. I read to them or they read to me. It's great fun. And I catch up on my reading at home."

"I hadn't thought of the school. Maybe the art teacher could use some help. I was an artist."

My God! That's the first time I've said 'was an artist' instead of 'am an artist.'

"Yes, I know," Farah says. "Someone told me to look around the pueblo at all the screens you've done. They are so beautiful."

"Thank you. I don't plan to make any more images like those. I'm trying to find something new to do."

"Well, I'm sure the school could use some help until you find something."

I smile. We sip tea for a minute or so.

"Farah," I say, "you seem to be such a happy person. Can you tell me the secret of your happiness?"

"Oh! ... I suppose I am happy, aren't I? Hmm ... I've never thought about happiness as being a secret. ... Well, ... when I look at most people, they don't seem as happy as I feel. I don't know how happy they are, of course. Someone might have a serious look on their face and be quite happy inside. Do you think that's true?"

"Yes, I suppose so. Is there something special that you do, that most of us aren't aware of?"

"Let me think. ... My mother was a very happy person. She lived for our family. She showed me that, if I could learn to love serving others, I would always be happy. She never said those actual words; she demonstrated it every day as my sister and I were growing up by the way she served the whole family. She encouraged us to serve each other and father."

I think about this for a while as I refill our teacups.

I say, "My parents served my brother and me, but they urged us to achieve something that would benefit the whole pueblo. However, it wasn't about the joy of service; it was more that we had a duty to the community. My brother became a doctor. You've seen my art, which may benefit the community. ... It doesn't feel that way to me."

"Well," Farah says, "we certainly have a duty to each other, but when we find joy in service, duty takes care of itself. Doesn't it?"

I take a sip of tea while I think about that. "I suppose it does."

« Huma »

It's mid-morning. I'm in the pharmacy, compounding a formula for a menopausal woman with typical symptoms. She prefers tablets, so I mix in a binding agent, then press the powder for each dose into oval pills. I put a month's worth of tablets into a brown bottle, affix a label, then set it on the shelf for her to pick up later.

There is nothing to do until another customer arrives. My screen shows no other prescriptions to fill at the moment. The pharmacy records are up to date. I sit down at my desk to double-check my emails in case a doctor has sent something in for me. Nothing.

My recent thoughts about the grief process wander through my mind. Playing with the idea of the long spiritual path that we metaphorically traverse, I imagine my life, the forty-five years so far, superimposed on a long, winding gravel road. I've never thought of it this way before. How have I been visualizing it? ... As a story, perhaps? As a dream?

The days of my life are laid in a row along this road, sometimes as rocky, hilly sections, sometimes in pleasant strolls through a level, sunlit forest. Along the trek are the changes — from a child to a teen, then to a young married woman, then to a pharmacist. Those changes were slow and gradual. The jarring change from a married woman to a widow took place in under five minutes. That part of the journey was like a cliff that I tumbled off when my mind was on something else. My comprehension of that change took place in one or two seconds.

"Huma, I'm sorry to have to tell you ..."

Recalling the rest of that sentence, I gasp. When I notice there was no exhalation, the breath leaves in a quiet groan, as when Jifah's boss stood at my door with that look on his face. That look ...

Beginning at the bottom of the cliff, this last year along the road seems more like a dark swamp than a hill or a sunny forest. Even though I've changed into a widow, I'm still a pharmacist. What does that mean to me? Who am I, really? Before Jifah died, the most important role in my life was being a partner in a marriage. During those years, I didn't understand how much that role defined me. But now my primary role is being a pharmacist. Is that all there is for me? I'll always be a pharmacist, but is there something else? — something that could become my primary identity? "Hi, I'm Huma. I'm a ..." What?

Fill in the blank, girl.

I consider changes that could be made. Thoughts flit through my mind like terrified birds that come in a window, fly around the room for a minute, then, finding the window again, are gone. I'm scared too. My mind is clouded with this lowering grief. There is no way to make a good decision now. There are little decisions, day by day — today I'll do this — tomorrow that. These aren't decisions about big life changes. They are ideas to play with for a few hours or days.

No decision is required today, or tomorrow, maybe not for years. At some point, the clouds will lift, then the decision will be clear.

‹‹ Mariha ››

Samat, Wertah, Amir and I are having dinner in our apartment, so we can all get to know Wertah better. I continue to be impressed with Wertah. He seems kind, polite, and treats Samat with a mixture of adoration and deference. She is pretty. Any young man would be attracted to her. I'm also impressed that he has learned sign language so fast. He is able to interpret for us, so we don't need the computer screens at the table.

I am resisting the urge to interrogate him. Perhaps Amir is also. There must be revealing questions that sound like polite dinner conversation.

"Samat tells us that you want to be a doctor." As I say this, Wertah signs it to Samat.

"Yes. I'm hoping to be a surgeon, but maybe I'll stick to wellness," he says and signs.

"You may want to talk to my mother, Dr. Khayat."

We pause while he signs.

"That would be great," Wertah says and signs.

"How did you meet Samat?" asks Amir.

"I was taking classes for sign language. Samat assists the instructor. She kept laughing at my mistakes. She's even prettier when she laughs. I asked her to have tea after class, so she could laugh at me some more."

Samat giggles at this. "His signing was so bad at first. He kept signing rude words by mistake. He's much better now. At least he's correct enough that I can guess what he's saying."

"I'm too old to learn another language," I tell him. "It's much easier to learn when you're young."

"You're not too old," says Wertah. "Now that the winter is coming, perhaps you'll have more time to study."

Samat says, "I would enjoy talking to you through signing, Mariha. It makes a difference. I can't explain it; it just seems warmer without the screen. I would help you study."

Tears are suddenly running down my cheeks. I don't know why. I reach over to hold her hand. She's looking at my lips as I say "Yes." Wertah doesn't need to sign my answer.

‹‹ Nadia ››

For the first time in over thirty years, I am sitting in the art class of the school I attended as a girl, to see how it feels to be an art teacher's assistant. Zuharah, the teacher, needs help. Today she has a dozen young teens making clay sculptures, their earnest young faces so intense, their foreheads wrinkled in concentration.

This will be fun. I'll get to play with all different forms of art along with them. Nothing will have my name on it. Nothing has to sell.

Education is free at the pueblo. In our culture, the children are the highest priority, so it is an honor to volunteer at the school. The full-time teachers are paid a salary, but there are many volunteers who assist them pro bono.

Zuharah introduces me to the class as an artist who has made many of the images that they see throughout the pueblo. She tells them that I am observing the class today to decide if I would like to volunteer. Their bright, eager faces smile at me briefly.

"Feel free to walk around," say Zuharah. "If you see someone struggling, you might offer a gentle suggestion, or better yet, ask them a question that could bring out their own solution, perhaps, 'What are you thinking about while you're working? Would a different thought, change the result?'"

I smile in agreement. We walk around the class. No one seems stuck, so I look for someone who is doing something interesting. It doesn't take long. A boy with shaggy hair and streaks of clay on his face is making a head about twenty-five centimeters tall. The head is screaming; it seems to be angry.

"That is extremely interesting," I tell him, "and very well done."

He stops to look at me.

"What's your name?" I ask.

"I'm Layan."

"I like your sculpture exactly as it is, but can you tell me why it isn't more placid? Most people would make a happy face."

"It doesn't feel real when I smile. Sometimes I need to yell."

"Yes, very good." My voice drops to a whisper. "You should be honest when you make art. It helps to know how you feel. If anyone criticizes it, tell them that Nadia likes it as it is."

Layan almost smiles, then goes back to work.

Later, while the students are cleaning up and storing their work, Zuharah walks over to me. "Does this seem to be something you'd enjoy?"

"Oh yes!" I smile. "I'd love it."

After the class, the school day is over for these students and teachers. Another group will attend the afternoon session. Some of the morning students take the elevators back to their apartments; others go to cafés or the school cafeteria. Zuharah invites me to eat with some of the afternoon teachers in the cafeteria. We join a group sitting at a long table.

"This is going to be such fun for me," I tell her. "Art has been a job for many years, becoming less and less fun each year. Recently I stopped producing new images until something enjoyable came along."

"I'm so glad to have you helping. Maybe something in the class will get your creativity sparkling again."

"I hope so."

« Huma »

I call Mariha to ask if she could use some company this evening. She asks if there is a problem. I tell her there is nothing in particular, only a need to be with her, to sit with her, maybe help Samat with her homework, anything.

Mariha's door is ajar when I arrive. I knock, then push the door open. Mariha is fixing the tea as I join them in the kitchen. Samat is at the table with her computer screen. We sit with her as she does her homework. At first I try to be quiet, but quickly realize that she won't hear our conversation. Samat is doing math, working very quickly, so she obviously doesn't need help at the moment. I reach for Mariha; she takes my hand and smiles.

I admire Samat's sweet face, no wrinkles, no blemishes. Her delicate mouth has hardly been kissed, but that will change soon. Her eyes sparkle with youth. She doesn't see my smile; she's concentrating. Samat's flawless fingers fly around her computer screen, tapping faster than my eyes can follow.

I sip my tea. As the cup returns to the saucer, I look at my hand. It is not a girl's hand or even a young woman's; it is weathered, wrinkled. It looks so old; if it weren't attached to my arm, I wouldn't recognize it as being mine. I must not have looked at it for a while.

I remember being the same age as Samat, with Nadia and Mariha — giggling girls at one of our apartments. As I reach for my teacup, there is my hand again; it looks like my grandmother's hand. It is the hand of a grandmother without grandchildren. Mariha must sense some part of my thoughts; she squeezes my hand. I look at her eyes. All the love we've shared for forty years seems to be looking back at me as she smiles. A tear trickles down my cheek. I smile back.

"I'm very happy to be here with you two ladies," I tell them, wiping away the tear.

Samat must sense something. She looks up at me, at my moist eyes. She looks at Mariha, who smiles and signs, "She's fine." The expression on Samat's face says that she is trying to understand what is going on with Mariha and her weeping friend. She doesn't ask. What would we tell her if she did? It has something to do with time and grief, something to do with friendship, something about being content with the moment. Mostly, it has to do with love.

Samat has switched to history. She's reading a text on her screen. Her forehead is furrowed with thought.

"This doesn't make sense," she says. "I'm reading about the Calamity. This says that before the Calamity, corporations were moving manufacturing around the planet to wherever there was the cheapest labor. That's impossible. No one would do that."

I pull out my screen, then open a chat window so I can talk to her while she reads it on her screen.

Huma: Why do you say that?

"Wouldn't they know the suffering that would cause? And besides, don't people all make the same wages for the same work?"

Huma: They do now. Back then, there
          was racism and nationalism, so
          corporations thought nothing
          of exploiting people in other
          countries who often didn't make a
          living wage. There were people who
          thought the only worthwhile goal
          was accumulating money.

"But what about a sense of community?" she asks. "Wouldn't the people produce the things they need in their community?"

Huma: The marketing by the corporations
          created a consumer culture
          where the people demanded more
          and more products at lower and
          lower prices. The people in rich
          countries thought they could

```
prosper if they made their money
by investing in the corporations
while the poorer countries did all
the manufacturing. At that time,
the corporations used big ships,
burning oil, to move products
around the world for a small
price. Once the fossil fuels were
exhausted, it all fell apart.
```

"That's the stupidest thing I ever heard. They deserved the Calamity for creating such a dumb system."

```
Huma:     Except it wasn't just the rich
          people who suffered. Even the
          poorest people died in wars or
          starved in the famines. If I
          remember right, there wasn't
          anyone on the planet that wasn't
          affected by the Calamity.
```

"When they saw that things were going badly, why didn't they change what they were doing? That's stupid."

```
Huma:     The people in power thought they
          were more important than the poor
          people. They had enough money
          to remain comfortable for many
          years, until everything fell apart
          completely. It was quite sudden.
```

Chapter 6

« Huma »

I'm spending a month in silence — as silent as possible. Nadia and Mariha are irritated by it, but they are supportive, nonetheless. We still meet in the afternoons. I smile at them as they talk. It was difficult the first few days. Afterward, my need to talk waned.

When I must talk, for instance, at work, it is very enjoyable. I savor the sounds of my clients' voices. The sounds of the pharmacy are like music — the rustling of the stock-person restocking the shelves; the murmur of the cashier across the room, speaking to a customer as they pay their bill; the sounds of the elevators and corridors. Every sound seems precious.

My apartment in the evening is a quiet oasis. I hear my breath, sometimes my heartbeat. There are the sounds of chewing and swallowing. I hear my thoughts, but they seem at a distance, as a quiet conversation in another room. The silence separates the useful thoughts from the nonsense. I love that.

As time goes by, there is less nonsense.

‹‹ Nadia ››

Zuharah and I are having lunch with the teachers in the school cafeteria. There is the usual chatter among teachers: how to reach problem students, what they'll do when they have some time off.

Zuharah and I sit across from each other nibbling sandwiches. She says, "You seem to have connected with Layan."

I nod while chewing.

She says, "I don't know how to reach him. He doesn't want to talk to me, but he listens to you. With me, he seems angry."

"I can relate to his anger," I tell her. "I feel frustrated myself."

"You?"

"We seem to have an artistic standard that all art has to be pretty. I suppose that works for public art — the stuff we put in a corridor or lobby — but some people are angry, and it helps to express that anger."

"If someone is angry, don't sculptures like Layan's make them feel more angry rather than less?"

"Not necessarily. When looking at his work, I feel as if someone else feels my frustration. I guess you could say it makes me feel happier."

"That doesn't make sense to me. When I look at a pretty image, I feel happier. If I were angry, looking at the same picture, wouldn't it make me feel happier?"

"Perhaps, but you might also feel lonely. Most people in our pueblo are happy; I only know a few people who aren't. Perhaps a sad or angry person feels lonely when surrounded by only happiness. If all the art they see is these vapid, happy pictures we commonly make, then they will feel alone in their sadness. If art were available that expresses anger, then they might think, 'Ah! At least someone knows how I feel.'"

"Layan's art makes happy people feel sad. It's negative," says Zuharah.

"That's probably true. I'm not suggesting that we should put Layan's work — or my recent work — on public display. It isn't for everyone. But it should exist in private spaces where people can explore different emotions."

"What kind of spaces?"

"Perhaps galleries that cater to more broad-minded people."

Zuharah looks shocked. She pulls back slightly in her chair, then glares at me. "I consider myself broad-minded!"

"Of course! Sorry, I shouldn't have used that word. You certainly are broad-minded, Zuharah. Don't misunderstand me. But there are people who wish to experience a wider range of emotions. That's true of me, too. I'm feeling frustrated, so art that expresses frustration would appeal to me. I wouldn't enjoy art that expresses violent anger or hatred. We all have our needs and limits."

"Art is permanent," says Zuharah, standing up. "Anger and frustration are not. Art should always express positive emotions and beauty."

I open my mouth to say something, but Zuharah has already turned away and stormed off. It is just as well; I didn't know what to say. If I had thought of something to say, it probably would have made her angrier.

« Mariha »

Samat is sitting next to me on the couch in the living room. She seems nervous; she is looking down and fidgeting with her hands. I take my screen out of my bag, then set it on my lap with a voice-actuated chat window open.

```
Mariha:    Samat, dear, is something
           bothering you?
```

"I'm ... uh ... Wertah and I want to get married after this school year." She takes a few deep breaths, then looks at me briefly, then back at her hands.

```
Mariha:    Yes. You told me that before.
           Let's talk about it. I hope
           you have thought about all the
           consequences. How sure are you
           that this is what you want? I'm
           sure you want to be with him now,
           but you know that you'll be with
           him for seventy or eighty years.
           That's a long time to care for
           someone.
```

"I think I'm sure. ... Is there some way to know?"

```
Mariha:    No. I wish there were, but there
           isn't. The big question is: will
           he be a responsible partner as you
           go through the many difficulties
           of married life? What about his
           parents? Are they happily married?
           Sometimes you can get a sense of a
           young person's future by looking
           at their parents.
```

"They are very nice, and I think they're happy, but mine aren't. What does that say about me?"

```
Mariha:    Well,... it says that you may not
```

> have had the best role models as
> you grew up. It doesn't mean that
> you will fail in your marriage,
> but it probably means that you'll
> have to try a little harder than
> another woman might.

I see that there is something else going on with her. She is still fidgeting. I wait for her to continue. I rub her hand as I wait.

She looks at me for a second, then down at her hands. "I'm going to have a baby."

I don't say anything. I put my arm around her to hug her shoulders, then kiss her hand. We sit for a few minutes in silence.

"I'm scared."

Mariha: I know. … You should not make the
          decision to get married because of
          the pregnancy. If you want to stay
          here, without getting married,
          you and I could raise the baby
          together.

"You don't think I should get married?"

Mariha: I believe Wertah is a good person,
          but you have to consider living
          seventy or eighty years with him.
          The baby will grow up. In twenty
          years, he or she will have moved
          to their own apartment. You'll
          still have fifty or sixty years
          with Wertah after that.

She studies my eyes for a minute while my words sink in. It's a little unnerving.

"What causes a marriage to fail?"

Mariha: Marriages don't fail very often, but, from what I hear, failure often has to do with a lack of contentment. A person who can accept the difficulties that we all face, overcome them to the best of their ability, then be content with the final result, will have joy in their life. That joy they'll share with their partner. However, if a man or woman can't accept the difficulties, they might blame others, maybe even their partner. They won't have as much joy to share. In the worst cases, the lack of contentment turns to resentment, which almost always destroys the marriage.

"How do I know if I'm content enough?"

Mariha: Sweetheart, I don't think you can learn that as a child. A child's life is relatively easy — even yours. As married partners live with each other, they experience difficulties together. Some they will overcome, some they won't. By struggling through the troubled times, they learn contentment. They help each other. I have confidence that you'll be able to learn it.

"Really?"

Mariha: You know what it is to struggle. Maybe Wertah understands it too. You'll have to decide as you get to know him better. I can promise

```
you this: I will always be here
to discuss your difficulties. It is
my hope that, over the years, we
become like mother and daughter.
```

"No matter what the problem is?"

```
Mariha:    Anything at all.
```

There are a few minutes of silence. I continue holding her hand, marveling at the perfect, translucent skin on the back of her hand.

"What's it like to raise a baby?" she asks.

```
Mariha:    It's wonderful. It's more fun than
           you've had so far in your life.
           But it's also a lot of work, and
           it strains the marriage. That's
           why it's best to wait to get
           pregnant, so the young couple has
           time to get used to each other,
           to truly fall in love before the
           pressure of caring for the baby
           creates stress.
```

"So we have made it harder than it had to be?" she asks.

```
Mariha:    Yes, that's true.
```

Another few minutes passes while she considers this, seeming to study the weathered hand holding hers, then looks up at my face.

```
Mariha:    Have you thought about where
           you'll live?
```

"Normally, newlyweds live with the girl's parents until they finish school. I don't know if my parents will be reconciled by then. I wouldn't want to move in with them until they are happy."

```
Mariha:    Amir and I will discuss whether
```

```
            you can continue to live here
            with Wertah and the baby. I can't
            promise you that without talking
            to him. When we agreed to take you
            in, it was a simple decision, and
            we were delighted to have a new
            daughter. But, to have another
            married couple living here, and
            with a baby too — well, you
            can see that situation is more
            complicated.
```

"I'm so sorry to bring this trouble on you," Samat says.

```
Mariha:    It's no trouble. I've been a
           little sad that my sons don't
           need me very much, so helping you
           through this — however it turns
           out — will be a welcome adventure.
           I'm sorry about this problem for
           what it means to you. You have
           been a gift and a joy. Amir and I
           love you, Samat.
```

« Nadia »

I am in the art class, standing by a huge table, two by three meters, where Layan and three other students are working on their clay sculptures. Layan continues to refine the head with the angry expression while all the other students in the room are sculpting animals, peaceful-looking people or abstract shapes. Two of the girls are sculpting a mother embracing a child — such a cliché. I don't say anything.

I want to appease Zuharah, so I mostly avoid Layan. He doesn't seem to need my help. I walk around the room, offering little encouragements to the others. A girl working on a woman's face stops me to ask why it doesn't look right. It is obvious that her proportions are a little off. I ask her to look closely at my face and measure where everything is. She makes a sketch, then jots down the measurements, so she knows the relationships between the eyes, ears, nose and mouth. Comparing the sketch to her sculpture, she sees the problem: the mouth is a little close to the chin and the nose is longer than it needs to be. I tell her she could consider keeping it as it is, as an abstract image. She says she wants it to look real.

Looking around the room, I see Zuharah bent over a table, working with a student. I want to say something to her, something that would show respect for her artistic sense. Yes, it would be dissembling. A believable lie doesn't come to mind, so I keep voicing my approval of the pretty sculptures among the students. Maybe that gets the message across.

« Huma »

In two days, my month of silence will be over. During the last few weeks, I have enjoyed sitting with Mariha and Nadia, listening to their conversation without having to think of something to say. It is tempting to continue the silence, but no; they want me to talk to them. They are frustrated when I sit there, smiling at them. During our last tea, Mariha said she feels as if there's a hidden secret when I smile at her. I smiled, looking down at my cup. We all laughed at my silent joke.

After the month is over, I will remain silent when alone. I have discovered that music was a distraction in the evenings. I thought it would be missed during this month, but it hasn't been.

My mind is quieter too. I'm able to be mindful, to focus on tasks, moment by moment. As Tamala told me on the beach, *live in the moment, no anger about the past, no fear of the future.* It's easier to do that without the mind chattering away.

I can still be absorbed by grief when I want to be.

Did I just say that?

Yes, ... sometimes I want to feel the grief, to remember Jifah and the love we shared. Maybe a tear or two runs down my cheek. But after a deep breath, a smile is possible, something about gratitude for the time we were given. There is a slowly lessening sadness that it wasn't longer, but also the realization that my sadness about these years of separation must not be allowed to overwhelm the joy of the years we shared. By accepting the situation, I'm living in the moment with gratitude rather than bitterness.

Wow! I should go back to Pensacola for another chat with Tamala.

‹‹ Mariha ››

Amir is looking at me as if I'm crazy. We're walking in the gardens below the building.

I tell him, "I thought it would be fun to have Wertah, Samat and the baby live with us."

"I don't have the patience."

"What would you prefer?" I ask.

We stop walking. He turns me toward him and takes both my hands in his. Looking down at our hands, he seems to be gathering his thoughts.

"I can handle Samat living with us during the pregnancy. After the birth, you'll enjoy helping her with the new baby, so I can probably endure living with a newborn for a year. After that, they can get married if they still want to. ... Or maybe they'll move into an apartment of their own before then."

"So you don't want them to marry and live with us?"

Amir says, "We don't have to make a decision now. Am I right? ... They won't get married before the end of the school year — about the same time that the baby is due. We can make the decision then."

"Right. We have time to revisit it."

"For now," says Amir, "we'll tell Samat that we want her to stay with us until the baby is a year old. We prefer that she waits until then to marry Wertah. If she insists on getting married after this school year, we'll discuss it at that time, but she'll probably need to find somewhere else to live with him."

"I want to think about that before talking to her."

I'm getting chilled, so, taking his arm, I turn us around to head back to the entrance.

Chapter 7

‹‹ Nadia ››

The art class is over for the day. As I'm walking to the elevators to go back to my apartment, I see Farah and hurry to catch her before she is swallowed up by the elevator.

"Farah! Hi! Do you have time for a cup of tea?"

"Well, ... actually I *am* hungry. ... Why don't you come to my apartment for lunch?"

A few minutes later, I am sitting at her kitchen table. She is preparing a salad while a pot of rice and beans heats on the stove.

"I'm feeling uncomfortable in Zuharah's art class," I tell her. "Her view of art is so different from mine. It is creating some tension, mostly in me. I'm forcing myself to conform to the rules she's teaching the students. If I could bring myself to believe in her rules, we'd be fine, but that's not possible."

Farah looks at me for a few seconds, then lowers her eyes to the salad as she mixes in the dressing.

"I can't have an opinion about art," she says, "but I can

imagine that the tension between you will be felt by the students. One of you will lose credibility, and it would be a shame if it were Zuharah; she's the one that has to teach year after year."

"I want the students to understand that there are multiple standards for art. It has been that way throughout history. There was never a time when the world agreed that all art had to look one way or have a single theme. It is only because we are so accustomed to the art produced in our pueblo that we consider our standard to be more correct than the standards of other pueblos."

"I don't know anything about art history," says Farah as she puts the food on the table, "so I'll assume that you're right about the multiple standards. However, do you want to fight the rest of the art community? Even if you want to start that fight, Zuharah's class isn't the place for it."

"You're right. ... Absolutely. ..." I take a few bites of the salad while I think about what Farah said. "I need to consult with other artists who may want to expand what we're doing."

"If you want to remain a volunteer at the school, perhaps you should look for another class to assist. All the subjects need volunteers. Try something you know less about, so the teacher won't see you as a threat to her authority."

"What a great idea." We both eat our salads for a minute. "You know, I've always felt bad about my poor sense of history. If one of the history teachers needs a volunteer, I can learn a bit myself."

"There you go. Talk to the vice principal. I'm sure she'll have a suggestion for you."

"Actually, art was the only subject I did well in. Any of

the other subjects will be a learning experience for me. I will definitely talk to the vice principal."

« Huma »

I'm taking the tube back to Pensacola to visit Tamala. It's turned cold at Whitetop, so it's a good time for a two-week visit to the Gulf. The scenery is fascinating as the capsule flies through the tube; the leafless trees are a grayish blur as we pass through the Blue Ridge mountains on our way south.

A few minutes later, the capsule stops briefly at the terminal for the Birmingham Pueblo, a truncated pyramid. People get off and on. The doors hiss shut. As we zoom farther south, the blurred scenery has patches of green. After we cross into what was once Florida, the blur is mostly green, less gray. Along the tube, as the capsule slowly approaches the Pensacola terminal I see pine and magnolia trees, live oaks with hanging moss, and, of course, Kudzu.

I walk a kilometer to the pueblo, then take an elevator to my rented apartment. After my things are unpacked, I call Tamala. There's no answer. I put on a light jacket for a walk around the gardens below the sphere. The weather is clear but cool. I make one lap around the building, enjoying the flowers and the people who are out walking. It takes an hour to go around once.

I buy a tea at a kiosk, then sit at a café table facing the entrance that Tamala normally uses. After a few minutes a girl, perhaps nine or ten years old, stops to talk.

"You're not from our pueblo," she says, looking at me with her head tilted to the side.

"No. My name is Huma. I'm from Whitetop — visiting for two weeks."

"My name is Mubakreh. Why are you sitting out here in that little jacket? Aren't you cold?" She sits down in the chair across from me. She's wearing a heavy coat and gloves.

"Your weather is much warmer than where I live. It feels good." I take a sip of tea. She seems to be waiting for me to say more. "Do you know a very old woman named Tamala? I called her, but there's no answer."

"Yes. She was my grandmother's cousin. She died three days ago. Her funeral was yesterday."

"Oh! ... I'm sorry. ... I hoped to talk with her during my visit. I came here once before, and found her meditating on the beach. She was very kind to me."

"And to me. She was very wise," says the girl. "I loved talking to her about her life. She had funny stories about when she was a girl."

"I loved talking to her, too. She helped me understand what was happening in my life."

"What was happening in your life?" she asks.

"Well, ..." I pause, looking for an appropriate answer to her inappropriate question, "my partner died, so I need to decide who I want to be now. Do you understand?"

"No, not really."

"When I was married, I thought of myself as half of the marriage. That's not possible now, so I need to see myself in a new way."

"Aren't you just yourself? ... I'm just myself."

"I hope it is that easy. ... Mubakreh, you are a wise woman. I will consider what you said."

We stand up, then say goodbye. I watch her walk away with a skip in her step.

I return my cup to the kiosk, then join other tourists who are waiting for the cart to take them down to the Old Pensacola exhibit.

« Mariha »

Samat is sitting next to me on the sofa in our living room. She is crying, dabbing her eyes with a tissue. "I thought I would live here with you, Wertah, and the baby. I need to have Wertah with me."

She watches the chat window on my screen as I talk.

```
Mariha:   I know how you feel. I was a young
          woman about to be married once.
          I wanted to be with Amir all the
          time. We want you and the baby
          here with us, but not Wertah. If
          you have to live with him, maybe
          you could find another apartment.
          I'll still help you with the baby.
```

"I don't understand what the problem is. Why can't Wertah be here too?"

```
Mariha:   Amir and I have talked about that.
          This apartment is too small for
          two couples. I'm sorry. Amir and I
          need some privacy and quiet. We're
          older. If we were younger, it
          might be different.
```

"Can you help me find another apartment?"

```
Mariha:   Certainly. We'll go talk to the
          council office about it. Now,
          let's talk about the best time
          to marry Wertah. Consider this:
          young couples, if they get married
          because of a pregnancy, often have
          problems with each other after the
```

> baby is born. If you wait until
> the baby is a year old, and you
> find that you still want to marry,
> then you'll have a better chance
> of being a happy couple.

"I want to live with Wertah now. I don't even want to wait until school is over."

Mariha: Of course you do. I was the same
way with Amir before our marriage.
It's hard to wait. But, you have
to consider how hard it will be
after the baby is born. There will
be more stress and less sleep. You
could end up fighting and hating
each other.

"Maybe you and I will fight and hate each other."

I smile at her.

Mariha: Maybe we will, but you won't have
to live with me for eighty years
afterward.

She laughs, then puts her arm around me, laying her head on my shoulder.

Mariha: Besides, I only want to help you.
After the baby comes, I'll be
there to help, not to control your
life.

"You think Wertah will control me?"

Mariha: Well, young women try to control
their men; young men try to
control their women. Older married
partners learn to support each
other without interfering with
each other.

"Can we talk to the council office tomorrow about an apartment for Wertah and me?"

```
Mariha:    We'll go tomorrow afternoon. Is
           that alright?
```

« Nadia »

It's eight o'clock in the evening. The dinner dishes are clean and put away. Radi is watching a film on the living room screen. I'm lying on our bed with the levitation turned off, looking at a list of artists who may resent the limits imposed on our work. I call each one to ask two questions: Are you happy with the art you're producing for sale? And, if not, would you enjoy getting together to discuss a new paradigm that might allow us more flexibility?

By nine o'clock, I've found that most are sympathetic, but not willing to change. Only two are willing to meet the following afternoon to chat.

Radi comes to bed. He points out that we haven't made love since we got the new bed. He wants to try it with the levitation turned on. I remember Mariha's story of her client trying to have sex in one of these beds. I smile while taking off my nightgown.

He gets into bed and switches on the levitation. We drift up a few centimeters.

"You have to hold onto me," I tell him. "There are funny stories about people flying around on these beds."

I feel as if I'm floating on a cloud. He starts making love, but with far too much energy. His legs are sliding around. Without his knees touching the bed to anchor him, he's thrashing around like a person on ice skates for the first time. There's a force field that surrounds the bed to keep us from falling out. We bounce against this field, which throws us across the bed to bounce again. The more Radi flails about, the more we ricochet off the force field.

"Slow down, dear. Wait for the bouncing to stop."

He does. Once we drift to a stop in one of the corners, we hold onto each other and make love with small movements that don't move us about so much. I am not sure that Radi will want to try this again, but at least my girlfriends will have something to giggle about the next time we meet for tea.

* * *

The next day at three, I'm laying out some snacks and tea on my kitchen table when the doorbell rings. At the door are Hazli, a tall, slender man with a gray ponytail, and Rian, a short, round woman. I like her; she's shorter and rounder than me.

I show them into the kitchen. After we sit down, all three of us remove a screen from our bags, then set them on the table so we can share images.

"I've been thinking for some time," begins Rian who pauses to sip her tea, "that my work is no longer satisfying. I was so happy to get your call last night. I've been afraid to show my clients anything unusual. I'm tired of being afraid."

"Same here," says Hazli. "I've played with some ideas, but have been reluctant to show anyone what I'm doing. In the past, whenever my work has wandered away from the norm, there have been blank stares or frowns, and certainly no sales!"

"I understand," I tell them. "Let's take a few minutes to share what we've been doing — the stuff that we are reluctant to show others."

I put some of my work on my screen and transmit it to

their screens. I tell them, "I've been feeling confined and angry, so you can see those emotions in these images."

"Wow!" says Rian. "They certainly look angry, but fascinating. I ... I am enjoying looking at them, but I wouldn't want them on my living room wall."

I laugh. "I suppose not. I don't put them on my wall either."

Hazli is smiling. He flips through some images on his screen. "Here are a few I've been working on."

Four images pop onto my screen. They are powerful graphics, abstract shapes with vibrant colors. The lines in the image are sharp, giving the impression that the images are photographs of real objects.

Rian says, "I love these. I would never have conceived images like them. This is exciting. These would look good on my walls at home." She sees my amused look. "No offense, Nadia. I'm glad to see your images, but they are best experienced in the moment, rather than long term."

"No offense taken, my dear," I tell her. "Yes, some images, like songs, are for a momentary experience, others remain pleasing for days or decades. Both are valid. Let's see some of yours."

Rian fusses with her screen, flipping through seemingly endless images. Finally she arranges three images, then pops them onto our screens. Each is a collage of other images. She has combined photos of real objects with graphics.

I look back and forth between Hazli and Rian, then say, "I'd love to have works by each of you on my walls — very impressive work. So ... where do we go from here?"

Rian says, "We should have a show. I don't care if none of this sells. We need to get this work out there."

Hazli nibbles on a cookie while he flips back and forth between my work and Rian's. He looks up at us. "Absolutely! We have enough work that the three of us could have a show. It'll start a conversation throughout the art community."

"That's what I want," I say, "a conversation. I want artists talking about art, not doing the same old thing ad nauseam. I'm sure there are artists who will join the conversation when they see the show."

Rian says, "That should be the title of the show, 'A Conversation'."

"Perfect! ... Let's talk to the gallery owners over the next few days," says Hazli, "and find someone who'll give us their space for a few days. Maybe we could have shows in more than one gallery with different images in each."

Based on who knew which gallery owner best, we divide the galleries between us, planning to get together in a week to check our progress. After they leave, while straightening the kitchen, I realize that I'm happy to be forming a friendship with Rian and Hazli. Having them to discuss art is going to open a new opportunity for joy.

« Huma »

The donkey cart arrives to take tourists down to Old Pensacola. It has a low bed with two wooden benches facing each other. There is a family with three children on one side, an elderly couple and myself on the other. The avenues around the Pensacola Pueblo are all gravel so the loudest sound, as the cart moves down into what was once the town center, is the crunching of the gravel under the wooden wheels.

The local council has recreated four blocks of the town. The buildings, none of them original, are all museums with reproductions of furniture that was used in the twenty-third century. The streets, once asphalt, have been replaced with concrete, stained black.

The cart drops us off at Palafox and Cervantes Streets. A sign says that the historic area is a modern reproduction based on photographs and records from 2275. It gives a brief history of the town from the earliest Spanish explorers in the sixteenth century to the building of the pueblo in 2568.

The family with children goes directly to a working reproduction of an ice cream parlor. The elderly couple stands with me while we read the sign. We each look at our computer screens to begin the walking tour, with a voice describing each building as we proceed down the street.

After four buildings, I'm finding the information repetitive. There was a hotel, then a restaurant, but the other buildings seem to contain only the offices of attorneys and insurance companies. I say goodbye to the couple, then return to Cervantes and Palafox to wait for the cart to take me back to the pueblo. There's a comfortable wooden bench on the sunny side of Cervantes, so I sit and wait, looking at the antique gold lettering on the windows of the building across the street, wondering why the earlier people would have needed insurance. The concept of insurance baffles me.

I wrap my coat tighter around me. It is a bit chilly, but not uncomfortable. There are five people on the corner opposite me. One of them is laughing, the others smile at her laughter. They are obviously friends.

I think about relationships. As the laughing people turn the corner, passing out of sight down a side street, a wistfulness for Nadia and Mariha washes over me. Friends ... hmm ... There is disappointment that Tamala has passed on; I wanted to talk to her. For a minute or two, I consider looking for another wise old woman to give me some guidance, but decide that it doesn't feel right. I will return to Whitetop, cutting my vacation short.

I look at the digital clock on a screen attached to the

bank building; there are another forty-five minutes before the cart will pass by on its way back to the pueblo. There's enough time to wiggle some beach sand between my toes.

« Mariha »

Samat and I are sitting in the council offices, looking across a desk at the housing administrator, a pleasant woman about my age. I tell her that, next June, we may need a two bedroom apartment for Wertah and Samat, either close to our apartment on the same floor or close to the elevators on a nearby floor. She types their names into a waiting list. She explains that apartments like that become available frequently, but she can't promise one for next June. She will let us know as the date gets closer.

Samat and I look at each other, then stand up. She thanks the woman. We head back to the apartment. In the elevator, she seems to want to say something.

"What is it?" I sign to her. It's one of the few signs I know.

"I've been thinking about our conversation yesterday. ... I think ..." she pauses.

"Go ahead," I sign.

"You're right about us waiting to get married. I got pregnant because Wertah was pressuring me. I trust him, but not enough to marry him in the spring. He'll be mad at me, but it's safer to wait until the baby is older. A friend of mine has a new baby. She said she didn't want to have sex for a long time after the baby was born. She was busy all the time and so tired. I can imagine Wertah pressuring me when I'm too tired for him."

I smiled, hugged her shoulders, then kissed the top of her head.

* * *

Fifteen minutes later, we are back in the apartment, sitting at the kitchen table with soft drinks. We have our screens before us, so we can have a deeper conversation.

Mariha: I can help you talk to Wertah if you want. If I tell him that Amir and I insist that you wait to get married, then he'll be mad at us and not you.

She frowns. "I don't want to lie to him."

Mariha: It's not really a lie; that is what we want. I know what you mean, though. What would be the truth? Maybe 'insist' is too strong a word. We could say that Amir and I feel strongly that it is best for you to wait. Then you could say that you respect our wishes. How is that?

"I love you, Mariha. You are so wise."

Mariha: Can I ask you a personal question?

"Yes, of course."

Mariha: Are you and Wertah going to have sex before the baby is born?

She closes her eyes for a minute or so. She sighs. "I know that he wants to, and I want to, but something feels wrong. What do you think?"

Mariha: For women, having sex confuses things. If you have sex with him in the next several months, you are going to be so in love with

him that you may not be able to
decide if marriage is the right
thing for the two of you. For
the next eighteen months, if you
remain friends, and spend your
time caring for the baby and
planning a future together, you
will learn more about each other's
character. This will give your
parents time to get to know Wertah
and his good qualities. Remember
they still have to give their
permission, even though you aren't
living with them. The council will
insist on their approval.

"Yes. If we behave ourselves during this time, my
parents will feel better about him."

Mariha: Have you told your parents about
           the baby?

"No. Not yet."

Mariha: You must tell them in the next
           month before the baby bump
           appears.

"I will."

Chapter 8

<< Nadia >>

Rian, Hazli and I are in Rian's studio, planning our shows. A gallery has agreed to give us their whole space for a weekend. There are two more galleries that will allow us to use their spaces if there is a good response to the first show. I'm feeling more excited with each passing hour. Maybe we are at the beginning of a new era in the art of our pueblo.

The first show will be the least radical, the second and third will move progressively away from the current standard. We are sharing images with each other, helping to choose the thirty-six images that will go in each show. Rian and Hazli have dozens of images to choose from. I barely have the twelve needed for the first weekend. I'm going to have to work hard to produce enough work in two or three weeks.

Looking at their work, I'm feeling stimulated — such a great feeling, and something not felt for a while. This is such a wonderful change from my recent artistic dilemma, the conflict with Zuharah, the response to my work at Fairy Stone, and, of course, my own inner turmoil about where to go from here with my work.

There is some joy surfacing. Instead of feeling as if there is nowhere to go with my art, I'm excited about the next steps. Each morning I'm anxious to get out of bed so my fingers can begin the next image.

« Huma »

I am back at my apartment at Whitetop. There are several days of vacation left, so I am spending the mornings in meditation and reading. When my meditation ended a few minutes ago, I started wondering about my next step as I continue the healing from Jifah's death.

It is time for lunch. In the kitchen fixing a salad, I'm recalling how much Tamala helped me by drawing from her personal experience with losing partners. Maybe it is possible to have similar experiences here at Whitetop. While considering the benefits of sharing our grief or fears with other widows, it becomes obvious that I need to start a support group.

What does it take to start one? ... Hmm ... It seems we need a place to meet and an announcement. After lunch, I walk down to the council offices to see when I can schedule a meeting in one of the community rooms. The building manager puts me on the schedule for the week after next. He tells me to send him a paragraph about the meeting, so he can put it in the community news that will display on everyone's screen each day for the week before the meeting.

As I walk back to the elevators, I think, that was easy.

« Mariha »

Samat and I are having afternoon tea with her mother, Talaq. We invited her to the apartment so Samat could tell her about the pregnancy. Samat and her mother sit together on the couch, a plate of cookies on the coffee table in front of them. I'm sitting in a chair across the room. We are all tense. Talaq must sense that something is wrong.

"Mother, I've made a serious mistake," begins Samat.

Talaq looks intently at Samat, then at me, her eyes searching mine for an answer. Our tension is turned up a notch. Talaq sets her teacup on the table, folds her hands in her lap, then looks back at Samat, waiting.

"I'm three months pregnant. I'm so sorry to add this to your worries."

Talaq's jaw drops open a little. She stares at Samat, her eyes moisten, then a tear runs down her cheek. I walk across to hand her a handkerchief.

"This is your fault, Nadia," says Talaq as she tears the handkerchief from my hand. "You were supposed to protect her." She signs at the same time so Samat can follow the conversation.

"Mother, Wertah and I never made love in this apartment. There was nothing Mariha could have done to prevent this."

Talaq gets up and paces the length of the living room. She signs while she says, "What are we going to do? Are you getting married? Are you finishing school? Where will you live?"

I hand Samat her screen. She opens a chat window. Her mother sits next to her, looking at her screen. I sit down in the opposite chair with my screen on my lap. I look at Samat for a moment, then speak into my screen, so she can see my words in the chat window.

```
Mariha:   Samat and I have been talking
          about that. With your permission,
          Talaq, she can live here until
          the baby is a year old. We've
          asked her not to marry Wertah
```

```
until then. You and I know how
stressful it is for a woman with
a new baby. Amir and I feel that,
by the time the baby is at least a
year old, Samat will have a better
understanding of her feelings for
Wertah and their future. You are
welcome to be here as much as you
can.
```

Talaq signs while saying, "Samat, what can I tell your father? He is already sick with worry about our marriage, and now this! He has to be told soon. ... Mariha, thank you for taking care of Samat. I was wrong to blame you. It was a stupid reaction. We will all work together over the coming months to help Samat as much as we can."

```
Mariha:   We will make a good team. And you
          will make a wonderful grandmother.
```

"A very young grandmother — I'm only thirty-two."

Samat says, "I may be a grandmother when I'm even younger than you."

Talaq smiles as she signs, "Yes. That will be your punishment!"

```
Mariha:   What did she say?
```

Samat chuckles. "She says I'll get what I deserve."

Talaq asks while signing, "Have you been to the doctor yet?"

"Yes. I have another appointment with Dr. Khayat in two days. So far, I've been doing well, just a little morning sickness, but that has already stopped."

Talaq is preparing to leave. She stands at the door hugging Samat.

I say, "I know this has been a shock for you, Talaq. Come

visit as often as you can. I'm sure Samat needs to spend more time with you, and I would enjoy getting to know you better."

« Nadia»

I'm sitting at my art table, looking at the dozen images chosen for the first show. I'm building up a little buzz with a second cup of strong tea. Twenty-two new images are needed for the second and third shows. There are three weeks to draw them.

The thread that runs through the twelve images is, of course, anger and frustration. While making them, I was struggling with the artistic boundaries. Now that I see the possibility of those boundaries changing, the anger seems to be gone. Now I'm ... what? ... maybe hopeful? excited? I've got to define my feelings if those emotions are to be revealed in the images.

An hour passes.

Finally! ... I have a theme — boundaries! The second show will be about boundaries, but with a sense of hope that they can be transcended. In the first set of images, my anger was about fixed limits, as in prison bars. My new boundaries will be like horizons, merely the limits of sight, not of possibilities. Remembering someone from art history, I search for Canadian women painters. Sasha Rogers was a twenty-first century painter who loved the interface between the physical and the spiritual, portraying it as a horizon. I flip through a dozen of her paintings to get me started.

This feels very good. I start to work on a simple image — just a horizon cutting through the middle with a dark foreground and a cloudy, but light-filled sky. As I work on it, adding some texture to the foreground, creating more definition in the clouds, other images are coming to me. I feel my soul stir again.

This is going to work!

« Huma»

My screen dings. I pull it from my bag and sit down at my kitchen table to answer the call. I don't know the woman calling.

"Hello."

"Is this Huma Nasik?"

"Yes."

"This is Joleh Resam. I saw the ad for the widows' support group."

"Yes."

"Well, ... I'm wondering if we can get together earlier. I'm a widow and have another friend who is a recent widow; she's truly struggling. I'd like to invite you to my apartment so the three of us can chat?"

"Sure. ... Yes, I'd enjoy that. When were you thinking?"

She chuckles. "I know this is sudden, but my friend is here with me now. Are you free at the moment?"

"I can be there in a half hour."

* * *

I knock on Joleh's door. A smiling woman about seven-ty-years-old opens it. We greet each other, then she leads me into her living room. Her friend is sitting on the couch with moist eyes and a handkerchief.

"Huma, this is Hazin."

The woman nods, then blows her nose. Joleh shows me to a chair opposite Hazin. She pours me a cup of tea, then places it on an end table beside me.

Joleh says, "My partner died last year. Hazin lost her partner a month ago. We've been talking almost every day since then. It's helped, so we're excited about a larger group."

"I'm excited too," I tell them. "I met a woman in Pensacola who had lost three partners. It helped me to share my experiences with her and hear her story. She was very old and very wise."

"Can you tell me ...," Hazin chokes, then starts crying again. Joleh puts her arm around her. We wait for her to continue.

Eventually Hazin says in a raspy voice, "Can you tell me how long this aching will continue?"

Oh my!

I say, "What the old woman in Pensacola told me was that it simply takes time. It never goes away completely, but we slowly get used to it so we can go on with our lives. How are you doing Joleh?"

"I'm getting used to it, as you said. Life is beginning to be enjoyable again. I laugh occasionally. He isn't constantly in my thoughts like he was at first. Lately, when he wanders into my thoughts, there's a little joy in the memory. I still cry, maybe once a week, but there's a sweetness at the same time. Does that make sense?"

I say, "Yes, it does. I'm about the same. Let us hope the new widows' group will help all of us, but especially new widows — give them some love while they express their feelings to people who have had similar experiences."

"Are we going to have a professional counselor in the group?" asks Hazin.

"We'll have to see who comes," I say. "Maybe we'll have a widow who is also a counselor, or maybe one of the women can recommend a counselor who we can invite."

Hazin says, "Is there something that I can do that will help me right now? Maybe something you've found that works?" She's looking back and forth between Joleh and me. I wait to see if Joleh has an answer, but she's waiting for me to talk.

"My friend in Pensacola said to focus on the current moment, not on the past. You'll remember your partner often enough, so don't *try* to think about him. Don't worry about the future either; that will usually create fear. Enjoy the present moment as best you can; feel Joleh's arm on your shoulder, sip the delicious tea, smell the candle or incense — whatever is making that lovely smell. Also, ... don't *avoid* thinking of your partner. Don't push him away; let the thoughts of him come when they want to come. Enjoy the memory, shed a tear if there is one, ... or smile in gratitude for the time you had together. But stay in the moment."

"I don't believe I can do that."

"Maybe not now," I tell her. "If you practice meditation, you'll increase your mindfulness. As you learn to stay in the moment, you will, more and more, enjoy those moments."

"It sounds as if meditation should be part of our meetings when the widows get together," says Joleh.

"I hadn't given any thought to the content of the meetings. You're right; we must include a meditation."

Joleh says, "Perhaps the three of us should work out an agenda for the first few meetings. After that, the whole group can adjust the agenda to suit themselves."

"Let's do that," I say.

We all take out our screens to begin a document that we

can edit together.

« Mariha»

I'm sitting at my kitchen table with Talaq and Samat. Earlier, we met with Dr. Khayat about the DNA procedure. I'm waiting for Talaq to say something. We've set out our screens and opened a chat window.

Talaq: The way I see it — my understanding of what Dr. Khayat said — is that we have to decide between letting the baby be born with her heart problem or attempting to modify her DNA to correct the heart problem.

```
Mariha:   Right. If we leave her DNA alone,
          she'll have a short, difficult
          life. She might live ten years,
          and she'll often be very ill. If
          we try to correct the DNA, there's
          a twenty-five percent chance of
          correcting it completely, but
          there's a seventy-five percent
          chance that the baby will be
          stillborn.
```

Samat is looking back and forth between her mother and me. She has tears pooling in her eyes. Talaq rests her hand on Samat's forearm.

```
Talaq:    I want Samat to make the decision.
          It's her baby. She's the one who
          will care for it.

Mariha:   Samat, do you know what you want
          to do. It's alright if you don't.
```

"I want to think about it for a few days and talk to Wertah. Today, I'd prefer to give her a chance at a normal life. If that doesn't work, and she dies before she's born, I feel that would be better than caring for her for ten years, then losing her. I need to pray about it."

Talaq: Mariha and I are here to help as
           you decide.

She kisses Samat on her right cheek. I kiss her left.

I'm struck by how much I love Samat. Having a pregnant daughter is different from having a son whose wife is expecting. There is something about the experience that mothers share. Her body is going through something that has happened to me three times. Although I've never experienced what will happen at the end of her pregnancy. She is so nervous. If nothing else, I can offer to sit with her as she visualizes what is happening inside her body.

Chapter 9

‹‹ Nadia ››

I am finishing the twelfth image for the second show. Each image is about some kind of boundary — time, space, or vision. The images for this show are supposed to be edgier than those in the first show, but these don't seem edgy at all. To me, they seem almost pretty.

I arrange them on the work surface, then sit looking at them for over an hour, trying to concoct a theme for the third show. Nothing is coming to me. I think the concept of boundaries is exhausted, at least for me.

I call Rian to see if we can meet this afternoon to talk. I'm hoping that she can pry some ideas loose from the dried mud of my brain.

She is happy to chat. I'm heading there now.

‹‹ Huma ››

Hazin, Joleh and I are sitting in a café on the twenty-seventh floor, watching the winter sun go down. The sky is beautiful, almost cloudless with oranges hanging over the mountains to the west. There is a dusting of snow on the harvested fields.

The three of us have met twice to experiment with the agenda. We have concluded that we need to start with each member talking about their recent feelings, then a fifteen minute meditation, then a thirty minute period when someone might give a talk, or some of us might ask the group for help solving a certain problem. The meeting will end with a social period.

There is still three days to go before the advertised meeting. Hazin and Joleh tell me they want me to chair the meeting. I'm nervous about doing it. I don't want to be seen as an expert with hundreds of widows coming to me for advice. Maybe, after the first few meetings, we can run them without a chairperson.

"I don't know about you two," I tell them, "but I'm feeling a little better after getting to know you and meeting in our small support group."

"It is helping some," says Hazin.

"Yes, a little," says Joleh, "but maybe that's all we can hope for. If we can feel that we're making steady prog-ress, maybe we will avoid depression."

I say, "Having you two as friends makes me feel better. I hope that when the larger group is established, everyone involved finds a few good friends within the group."

‹‹ Mariha ››

I answer a knock at my door. Talaq is standing there. Samat steps from behind me, draws her mother inside, then wraps her arms around Talaq's neck.

"Thank you for coming, Mother."

Talaq smiles nervously. The three of us go into the

kitchen, then lay our screens on the table. Samat asked to meet with us to discuss her decision. We know we will need a chat window.

The tea service is already on the table. I pour three cups, then look at Samat.

She looks at us both, then says in her loud monotone, "I've decided to have her DNA corrected. I know that chances aren't good that she will survive, but I believe it's her best chance for a happy life. I've talked to Wertah about it. He agrees."

```
Talaq:    It's a wise choice. I tried to put
          myself in the baby's place. If she
          dies before birth, she will be
          enveloped in the love of God and
          never know sadness. If she lives,
          she will have a normal life.

Mariha:   Yes, a very wise choice. Your
          mother and I will be right with
          you every day, regardless of the
          outcome.
```

Samat smiles, "Thank you."

She squeezes our hands.

```
Mariha:   Did Dr. Khayat say when the
          procedure is scheduled?
```

"Yes," says Samat, "it will be early next week. We have to go to Fairy Stone. There is a DNA specialist there that is qualified. It's such a rare problem. Dr. Khayat said this is the first case at Whitetop in ten years."

```
Mariha:   Talaq, do you mind if I come
          along? I'd like to be there.
```

« Nadia »

I have a new direction.

When Rian and I met two days ago, we wandered through archives of art from the last thousand years. I found something that truly excited me. Eight hundred years ago, there was a little-known artist named Eva Borowski. She made very colorful images based on crystals, mirrors, shiny spheres, and butterflies.

I am sitting alone at my worktable, with nine of her pieces laid out. They are amazingly joyful. Borowski's work would probably be accepted in our pueblo's current standards. There's nothing radical here, except that they are jubilantly joyful and photo-realistic.

Remembering about our original plan for the three shows, I chuckle. They were supposed to be progressively edgy and radical. My work seems to be going in the opposite direction. Therefore, I decide to put the twelve "boundary" images in the first show, saving the twelve "angry" images for the second or third show.

Basing my images on Borowski's work will be a challenge because I'm so used to making dreamy, soft-focus images. Of course, simply copying her work is out of the question. I must first find some happiness, then let that flow out of me through my interpretation of her style. Sitting here looking at her images, I'm almost happy enough to begin working.

Isn't it interesting that her images make me happy? I remember my conversation with Zuharah about whether sad people need to see happy images. Perhaps she was right.

None of my angry images made, or make, me happy. They are pretty, pleasant perhaps, artistically balanced in form and color, but, looking at them now, I feel dull. I think I felt dull when they were made. They are technically good but didn't come from a joyful place inside me. I need to find that joyful place if there is one.

I'll call Huma and Mariha to see if we could meet for tea this afternoon. We've all been so busy lately.

‹‹ Huma ››

I'm sitting in a café waiting for Nadia and Mariha. It's been a few weeks since we've met for tea. The weather is too cold to sit in the gardens.

The server brings a pot and three cups as Nadia waves to me from the door. She looks great, very happy.

"Why the big smile?" I ask as I stand to kiss her cheek.

"Isn't seeing you a good enough excuse?"

"Then I should be smiling too. ... Oh! There's Mariha."

We remain standing to greet Mariha, then settle into the booth to pour our tea. The server comes by to see if we need anything else. We don't.

"Let's hear all the news," says Mariha.

I say, "Two other widows and I are starting a widows' support group. You've probably seen the announcements on the morning news. We're meeting for the first time this weekend. It's going to be wonderful. I also went to Pensacola again to talk to my friend, Tamala. I told you about her. Anyway, ... she died a few days before I got there, so I came right back. But it was still a good experience. I walked around the old city for a few hours, then wiggled my toes in the sand."

We all look at each other, sip our tea for a while, waiting for someone to talk.

Nadia says, "You know how I've been struggling with my art? Well, ... two other artists and I have been talking about new standards. This is so great! We're going to have three shows in the next month or so. The first one is next week. You two have to come! I've got twenty-four images ready for the first two shows. The work on the third group of images is just getting started. For the first time in years, I'm happy with my work."

"Wow!" says Mariha. "You two are doing great! I'm so pleased."

She pauses, sips her tea, then realizes we are waiting for her to continue.

"Oh! ...," says Mariha. "What's new with me? ... Well, Samat is three months pregnant. That has been a bit of an experience. The baby has a rare genetic problem, so we're going to Fairy Stone next week to get it fixed. It's a very risky procedure, so please keep her in your prayers."

"How are you doing? Are you happy?" asks Nadia.

"Well," says Mariha, "... doing fine, I guess. Samat has given me a chance to be a mom again. That's been great. I love her. Her mother, Talaq, and I have become friends. I love that too. We'll work together to help Samat through her pregnancy."

"Is she going to get married?" I ask.

"I've told her that she can't get married if she wants to stay with us. She's applied for an apartment in case she and the baby's father want to get married at the end of the school year. I'm hoping she'll stay single and live with me until the baby is a year old. After that, she can make a better decision about marriage. Her mom feels the same."

"Please call if I can help," I tell her.

"Same here," says Nadia.

"Nadia, why did you want to get together today?" I ask. "You sounded anxious."

"I needed some inspiration for my art! My next dozen images are going to be very happy images. They need to come from a happy place inside me. A cup of tea with the two of you is just what I need to find that place. You both fill me with happiness; you always have."

"What a beautiful thing to say," says Mariha.

I reach across the table to grasp their hands. We look at each other for some time, then go back to drinking our tea.

« Mariha »

Talaq, Samat, and I are on our way to the DNA specialist. We are in the tube, flying to Fairy Stone, passing blurred grayness for fifteen minutes. From the terminal, we take a donkey cart to the pueblo. We are all shocked at how different it looks from our own. This is the first time any of us have left Whitetop's glass sphere. Before us is a foliage-covered, half pyramid. To me, it looks like one of the Aztec or Mayan pyramids that were found covered with jungle.

We enter the foyer, then ask directions at an information desk. We make our way to the elevators, then to the fourth level. As we exit the elevator, I'm struck by the long hallway, which seems endless. We walk past dozens of doctor's offices until we reach our destination.

A nurse takes Talaq and Samat into a procedure room while I sit in a small waiting area, browsing for the latest news on my screen. There are reports from teleconferences about every imaginable subject. I look through the summary of a teleconference that I was unable to attend. One of my attorney friends from Whitetop presented a document that described the software we developed to translate ancient legal documents into the international language we use today.

I only read a few paragraphs before Talaq and Samat

return. Samat has a smile on her face.

"That's it?" I ask and sign.

"It was easy. I put on a gown, then laid on the table. The doctor had this machine that he placed around my stomach. I didn't feel anything at all."

The doctor comes out a few minutes later to tell us the procedure seemed to work normally. He'll call Dr. Khayat, so she can follow up with us. He says that next month Dr. Khayat will be able to determine if the procedure was successful.

"Do we need to make another appointment with you?" asks Talaq, signing so Samat can follow.

"That's not necessary. Talk to Dr. Khayat. She'll let me know if any further procedures are necessary." Talaq translates for Samat; then, we thank the doctor and leave.

In the foyer on the first floor, we sit on a wooden bench to wait for the donkey cart that will take us back to the terminal. The cart's schedule is arranged so it arrives at the terminal a few minutes before each tube is due. About ten minutes later, we are told the cart is ready for us.

We walk out into a cold wind. The cart is pulled by two donkeys, one young and solid gray, the other older with a white face and tired eyes. We step up into the cart, then settle onto one of the two benches that face each other. Since it is winter, there is a canvas cover over the cart for warmth. There are eight of us in the small cart, so it is rather cozy.

During the tube trip back to Whitetop, Talaq signs, "How are you feeling about everything, Samat?"

"I expected some answers, I guess. It's almost as if nothing happened. And I'm disappointed that we have to wait a month to find out if it worked."

At the tube terminal at Whitetop, another cart is waiting to take us back to our pueblo. We ride in silence except for the thunk-thunk of the wooden wheels as they roll over the gaps in the flagstone.

Chapter 10

« Nadia »

It is late spring. Sitting at my worktable with a new image displayed on the glass, I'm stuck.

The three art shows with Rian and Hazli went well. The art community is excited about what we presented. The artists are buzzing with new ideas — some of them anyway. We seem to have broken through the stagnation that has plagued us for ... well, ... for as long as I've made art, probably longer.

I want to continue the sequence of happy, colorful, crystalline images that I used for the second show. However, it has grown progressively more difficult; it feels as if I need to go deeper into my soul. Finding inspiration for new images isn't as easy as during my first thirty years. Then, I could produce an image without giving it much thought.

Whenever I approach this new work in the easy-going mindset used before, the image turns out as a dull copy of Eva Borowski's work. I have to find my innermost joy, then hold that feeling while the image forms under my fingers. If my mind wanders, the connection with the joy is lost. I can keep the connection sometimes, but not consistently. I have to learn to hold onto those moments long enough to finish an image without slipping into regrets from the past or freezing in fear of some future tragedy.

« Huma »

I'm sitting on the couch with Hazin in Joleh's apartment. Joleh is sitting across from us in a chair. We are talking about the widow's group. There have been over a dozen meetings of the group so far. Thirty women are regularly attending. Other women show up from time to time.

As usual, we are talking about our feelings. Hazin is getting better, so is Joleh. I'm doing a fair job of staying in the moment during the day. The evenings are a little harder, maybe because I'm by myself in the space where Jifah shared my life.

When talking to another widow, I find it even easier to be in the moment. I try to be present for her, to love her and listen closely to her pain or joy. At those times, it is good to get outside myself for a few minutes.

Hazin says, "We always talk about staying present in this perfect moment, enjoying the good people and activities around us. OK, ... sometimes I'm able to do that for a few minutes, but then fall into a black hole of despair whenever a memory of my partner appears. The thought that I'll never see him again devastates me. Remembering the fun we had brings on the worry that I'll never have that much fun again."

Joleh says, "We can't beat ourselves up because we aren't able to stay in the moment all the time. If we do, it'll make us so unhappy that we'll never move on. We have to acknowledge that we are learning, that we aren't yet where we want to be, but we're moving along at a rate that's perfect for us."

I say, "Right! We are making progress! We can applaud ourselves for the perfect rate of improvement. During the times when we are present in the moment, we can celebrate our joy."

"At this moment," says Joleh, "I'm feeling love for both of you, and gratitude for this conversation."

Joleh comes across the room to kneel in front of Hazin. She puts Hazin's hand in mine, then holds our other hands.

"Let's truly feel this moment," she says. "Let it be like a prayer. Feel love, acceptance, hope, joy — whatever is in your heart will be perfect for this moment."

After two or three minutes, we squeeze the hands we're holding and look into our friends' eyes.

I say, "When we are together like this, it's easy to enjoy the moment. When we are alone in our apartments, it can be harder; we slip into our grief or experience fearful thoughts of the future. We can train ourselves, so when we lose our joy, we simply breathe while remembering the perfection of the moment. We only grieve or fear the future when we forget that we are living in a perfect moment, so just breathe."

Hazin asks, "What do we do if something painful is actually happening? We can't pretend that it's perfect."

Joleh says, "Even then, if we breathe while focusing on the present moment, we'll be able to think clearly so we can solve the problem. We probably know how to fix the problem if our minds aren't clouded by fear or grief."

I say, "I believe that's right. Each difficulty, even each negative thought, can act as an alarm bell that reminds us to stay in the moment, breathe, then solve our real problems, if any. Maybe we can even celebrate the alarm bells."

« Mariha »

Talaq and Samat are sitting with me in Dr. Khayat's office. We can tell from the doctor's face that she doesn't have good news. I can sense the tension in all of us.

Finally, she speaks, "I'm sorry. The procedure to correct the DNA of your baby wasn't successful."

Samat gasps, then moans as she exhales.

"What are the options?" asks Talaq. She is signing the conversation for Samat.

"The baby is alive. I expect it will be born normally, but will not survive outside Samat's body. It will die within hours. There's nothing we can do medically at this point."

Samat is sobbing; her shoulders are shaking. Talaq and I start to cry with her. When Talaq is able to regain her composure a little, she says, "Is there something non-medical?"

"There's nothing that will change the outcome. Remember that there is a spiritual connection between mother and child. The DNA problem can't damage that. Samat and the baby have only these few weeks together, so don't spend them in sadness. Be grateful for each day, each moment. Don't waste them in fear of the future or anger about the past. Don't think 'Oh, if I had only done this, or that, then the baby wouldn't have this problem.'"

The doctor continues, "Most mothers have sixty to eighty years with their daughters. Samat will have only the nine months plus a few hours. I'm sure she will fill these hours with love, compressing a whole lifetime of affection and caring into the little time she has with her baby. This will take concentration and focus on everyone's part. We can't expect Samat to enjoy these few joyful hours with her baby if her mother and friends are sad. Everyone must be joyful and celebrate the short time available."

I had tried to prepare myself for this, but I am a mess of tears. Talaq is also weeping, but is able to thank the doctor and assure her that we will do our best. Samat tries to say something, but her throat doesn't work. The three of us stand up and hug each other. I notice that Dr. Khayat is wiping her eyes.

« Nadia »

It is late spring. Having spent the last several months improving my technique, I can produce images that are almost photo-realistic instead of dreamy soft-focus. I have several sketches with ideas for new images that can be produced once my skills are up to the task. I'm very happy. It feels as if I'm moving forward.

I'm on my way to the gardens to have tea with Huma and Mariha. The elevators are full of people who have finished their morning work and are ready to enjoy the gardens on a clear, warm day. When the elevator doors open, the crowd of people streams through the foyer, then into the sparkling air outside.

I start walking along the path. Every table and bench is full. Moving along, I pass our usual table on the south side of the gardens. After fifteen minutes, I see them, standing at a kiosk, buying their tea. I join them. The three of us sit on a sunlit bench to chat.

"You seem happy," says Mariha.

"I am happy," I say, "but tired of cold weather. I'm ready for summer."

"Your work is still going well?" asks Huma.

"Very well," I say. "I'm excited to start every day. Ideas are flowing, and my technique is improving. ... Mariha, how is Samat doing?"

"The baby is due any day."

"How are you preparing for what is going to happen?" asks Huma.

"I don't know how to prepare for a birth and a death. It would almost be better if we didn't know that the baby will die. Dr. Khayat said we should compress the love of a lifetime into the few hours that we'll have with her. We're calling her Joharah. Talaq, Samat and I have been praying for her each evening. We sit on the sofa together with Samat in the middle, so we can each feel the presence of the baby while we pray."

"That sounds ideal," says Huma. "I'm sure Joharah can feel the love. That's the most important thing."

"Tell us what we can do," I say. "Can we be there to help when the baby arrives?"

"I hope you can both join us," says Mariha. "We don't know if the baby will live for a few minutes or a few hours. If the baby lives for a while, it would be so helpful if you could help with food. Even though we're trying to be positive, I'm sure we'll be emotional wrecks."

"My mother is planning to be there, along with the midwife," I say.

"If nothing else, we can be praying in the living room," says Huma.

"You can keep Wertah company," says Mariha. "He's planning to be there."

« Huma »

After drinking tea with Mariha and Nadia, I walk around the gardens. Throughout the last several months, I've been practicing mindfulness, savoring the present moment while letting any grief from the past evaporate whenever it arises. However, the birth and death of little Joharah will be a test.

I remember when Mariha and Nadia had their babies. We were all so excited, looking forward to playing with the new baby, anticipating first words and steps, birthday parties, and all the other events of childhood. With Joharah, there will be none of that.

The widows' group is thriving. Everyone says that it's helping them. Wonderful friendships have formed within the group. Everyone feels loved. It would be nice if there were such a group for young mothers who have lost a child, but children die so rarely. I doubt if there's another mother in the pueblo who is grieving for the recent death of a child.

« Mariha »

Samat is in labor. It seems to be progressing normally. Dr. Khayat, the midwife and Talaq are with her in the bedroom. Nadia, Huma, Wertah, Amir and I are in the living room, alternating between saying prayers and talking. It's almost midnight.

There is a strange calm in the living room. We know what will happen soon; the exact times of the birth and the death are the only questions. At any other birth, there might be anxious questions: the number of toes perhaps, or whether there's a birthmark or something else out of the ordinary. With Joharah, we know that the number of toes is irrelevant.

I fix a tray with two cups of tea and a glass of ice chips

for Samat, then walk to the doorway of the bedroom where Samat is floating in the birthing tub, breathing deeply. There is barely enough light in the bedroom to see them. I set the tray on a table behind the tub. Dr. Khayat is on one side of Samat, the midwife on the other. They are softly offering her encouragement as they keep the warm water flowing over her shoulders and wiping the sweat from her face. The scene reminds me of the birth of my children, such a pleasant memory, such joy.

Dr. Khayat tells me there's probably another hour before the birth. Samat is gripping the sides of the tub; she is having a contraction. I want to do something, but there's nothing to do. Sitting next to Talaq on the edge of the bed, I put my left arm around her shoulder, and hold her right hand with my right.

After five minutes, I return to the living room to join the prayers with my eyes closed. I don't feel like praying. As the sound of the prayers soothes me, my gratitude increases for the support that everyone is giving Samat. She'll need it in a few minutes.

I'm even grateful for this experience. People are so healthy today. Babies rarely have any problems. Normally, women live at least ninety years. They struggle through puberty and motherhood. They develop a profession. It's rare for a woman to live only a few hours, struggling to breathe. Little Joharah will have less struggle than the rest of us. Even though her brain will be starving for blood, she may not know that her tiny body is fighting for its life; for her it will be the way life is. Maybe she will be grateful for her few moments, not knowing that she's about to lose consciousness and die.

I think about my forty-five years of life and the forty-five more that await me. Joharah will have minutes. Are my years better than her minutes? Who could judge?

We hear some splashing coming from the bedroom. Joharah cries a little. For some minutes, we hear movement, then Talaq appears in the doorway and beckons us. Dr. Khayat and the midwife leave the room and go to the living room to rest. The rest of us move to the hallway, then stand outside the bedroom.

Samat, looking tired but radiant, is in bed with Joharah. The infant is wrapped in a white blanket. We enter in silence, then line up on either side of the bed. Huma kneels down. It seems the right thing to do. We all kneel. Something sacred is happening.

Samat looks around at each face and smiles. She looks tired but angelic. Each of us reaches out to touch her arm or leg. No one speaks.

She pulls the blanket back a little, so we can all see Joharah's face. She is exactly what I expected, a pretty little girl with a tuft of black hair the same color as her mother's. She's asleep.

After some time, we leave, one by one. When everyone is back in the living room except Talaq, Dr. Khayat goes back in to check on the baby.

We hear Talaq cry out, then start to sob.

Chapter 11

<< Nadia >>

I am walking down the hill from the cemetery. My arm is linked with Huma's. Talaq and Mariha are in front of us with Samat between them. Our partners and Wertah are behind us with the rest of the families.

The casket was so small. I can't get over how small it was. I don't know what I was expecting.

The women, Wertah and Amir walk back to Mariha's apartment. The others go about their day. There is tea, and sandwiches in case anyone is hungry. No one is.

We have striven during these last months to be positive for the baby, so she was enveloped in love and joy during her few months of life. Now we will support Samat as she gets used to being neither pregnant nor a mother.

We are sitting in the living room. Huma chants a beautiful prayer that begins, "O God! Refresh and gladden my spirit ..." That begins a round of prayers. I open a chat window on my screen so Samat can see what is being prayed. Most of the prayers express gratitude.

« Huma »

I keep recalling my dream about Jifah. He hasn't visited me in other dreams. He said that he doesn't feel any separation from me. Remembering him, I try to feel the closeness that he must feel.

His corpse is, by now, quite deteriorated in the grave. Once so alive and fun to be around, his presence is now a distant thought. For some reason, the recent memories are less clear than those from long ago: when I met him at thirteen, when we married at sixteen, when we made love for the first time.

Everything about him is distant except for his words in my dream. That is the new reality of him. He is present in a form I can't see. He sees me in a way that I can't understand. When I meditate now, I can feel him around me, not beside me, but around and through me, like the air in and out of my lungs, like the breeze on a warm day, cooling my skin, or the sun on a chilly day, warming me with loving kindness.

« Mariha »

Samat, Talaq and I are in Samat's bedroom. Samat, wearing a jumpsuit, is leaning against the headboard. Her mother and I are sitting on the side of the bed. Amir is in our bedroom watching the news.

"I have decided not to marry Wertah," says Samat.

"I see," signs Talaq.

I pull out my screen and open a chat window.

```
Mariha:    I'm surprised. What made you
           decide?
```

"Dr. Khayat told me that there's a possibility of our other children having the same problem as Joharah. Besides, I don't believe I love him now. He's a nice looking man.

He can find another woman to have healthy children with."

Talaq pulls out her screen.

```
Talaq:    Samat's father and I would like
          her to move back home. We have
          worked through our issues, so
          we're much happier now.

Mariha:   I'll be very sad to see her go.
          It's been a wonderful experience
          having her with us.
```

"I'm fifteen now. It's time for me to marry. Of course, I have to find someone first. Are you and Daddy ready to have me live with you and bring a partner into your apartment? If not, there's an apartment available for me. Mariha and I put my name on a waiting list months ago. I don't need to burden either of you. I could move into my own apartment."

```
Mariha:   You are no burden. I feel like
          you're my own daughter.

Talaq:    With or without a partner, you're
          welcome to come home if you
          want to. Your father and I will
          understand if you want to stay
          with Mariha. If you'd rather have
          your own apartment, we'll try to
          work that out.
```

"Can I think about it for a while?"

```
Mariha:   Wherever Samat decides to live, I
          hope the three of us can remain
          friends. Over the last months,
          both of you have become my family.
          I'm looking forward to knowing you
          both better.
```

« Nadia »

I am at my worktable, finishing the last image for a one-person show. These are so much better than the first set of "crystalline" images made for the previous show. Each image is based on the idea of looking into a multifaceted jewel that breaks up the image and introduces rainbows of colors. The name Joharah means "jewel" so there seems to be some connection between Samat's baby and these images.

The new images require more spiritual focus than my previous ones. I can't simply rely on some old formula and dash off an image. These images come from inside me, from some tender point of joy and gratitude.

Among our art community, there is an excited conversation in the cafés these days about the future of our art. I'm delighted to be a part of the conversation. The art of our community remains pretty, but now the artists are stretching their creativity, competing with each other to invent new approaches to beauty. This is exciting.

I ran into Zuharah at a gallery a week ago. She told me how much she enjoyed my new work.

« Huma »

It's a summer afternoon. Joleh and I are having tea in Hazin's apartment, which faces the northwest from the 156th floor. Out the window are bright green fields stretching to the blues of the distant mountains.

Hazin is happy. The widows' group has been meeting for several months. She is working hard and sharing what she learns with more recent widows. As new women arrive, Hazin shows great compassion and takes them under her wing, often bringing them to our afternoon teas.

Between these visits, and those with Mariha and Nadia,

I'm happy — so happy. I'm still meditating and learning mindfulness. It seems to be an unending process, always with another level to attain. My thoughts of Jifah are increasingly joyful, full of contentment. There's still a tear every once in a while. Tamala said there would be. I can be at peace with that.

‹‹ Mariha ››

Samat decided to stay with me, but she spends many evenings with her parents. The three of them seem to be getting along very well. She has taught me enough sign language that we can often talk without the chat windows.

Talaq, Samat and I are watching a movie on the living room screen in my apartment. Amir is watching something in our bedroom.

"I met a nice man," signs Samat.

"Go on," I sign, smiling.

"His name is Najar. He's a plumber's apprentice."

Talaq smiles. "It would be good to have a plumber in the family."

"When will we meet him?" I ask.

"He hasn't shown much interest yet. But maybe he's a little interested."

"Have you seen Wertah recently?" I ask.

"I see him in the corridors. He has a new girlfriend."

"I hope he is happy," says Talaq. "I liked him."

"Yes," I sign.

We sip our tea for a while.

Talaq asks while signing, "How about you, Mariha. Are

you happy?"

I bring out my screen so I can express myself clearly.

Mariha: I wasn't until you loaned me your
          daughter. I didn't realize how
          much I wanted a daughter all these
          years. Sons love their mothers
          but can't seem to be friends
          with them. Samat is so precious
          to me. I'm looking forward to
          the laughter and chaos that her
          children will bring to my life.

Epilogue

The Year is 2953, C.E.

Society Today

In the eleven hundred years since the nineteenth century, a world consciousness has evolved that celebrates, not money, property, and power, but, the essential oneness within the diversity of our human family. Those of us alive at end of the third millennium recognize the debt we owe to the millions who struggled in the nineteenth, twentieth and twenty-first centuries to awaken the planet to the dangers of the industrial age and the benefits of a sustainable civilization. We owe an even greater debt to the many who died in the wars throughout the Calamity as the obsolete power centers fought to hold onto their power.

Even though we can read about their struggles, we can only dimly imagine what it must have been like to live in such a primitive culture, one driven by fear and greed. If there were not video records of the time, many of us would doubt the written descriptions of their sacrifices.

All the basic structures of our civilization have been vastly improved since the industrial age; we are now more focused on our community than on our nation. When we think of our citizenship, we are primarily concerned with our local community. The nation states no longer govern in the sense that they did in the twentieth century; today they exist primarily for consultation and coordination.

Our communities are largely autonomous and self-sufficient. Most of us live in pueblos, a term we use both for our communities and for the single, large buildings in which most communities live and work. The buildings are permanent structures housing approximately 100,000 people with their businesses, schools and all other services. They are spaced at least 200 kilometers apart, providing adequate surrounding farmland and other natural resources for the needs of the population. Depending on the climate, the pueblos may be concrete, adobe, or glass and steel. All are designed to be lighted, heated and cooled with minimal external energy.

Today, ownership of any kind of wealth or property, whether by nations or individuals, is far less important than it was during the industrial age. The need to own or control is considered a childish fear left over from the time when mankind incorrectly believed there were not enough resources, and therefore hoarded property and wealth.

The world population is stable at less than 3 billion. There are approximately 20,000 average-sized pueblos in the temperate and tropical areas of the globe. A few larger ones exist, as do smaller ones. Villages, not unlike those of the industrial age, are located where people choose to live in mountainous or frigid areas. The drop in the planet's population, from a peak of 11 billion, was due to cancers and other industrial diseases, combined with chemically-induced infertility, between the years 2000 and 2300.

Perhaps the biggest change since the industrial age has been the increasing leadership demonstrated by women. Between 2100 and 2300, the role of women in all levels of society increased dramatically. Today, there are slightly more women than men involved in the pueblo and national governments. The infusion of the attitudes and qualities of women into the world culture is thought to be a major factor in the evolution of a world consciousness devoted to progress through cooperation, and a rejection of the survival-of-the-fittest mentality that dominated earlier cultures.

The concept of prejudice bewilders most people today. It is difficult for us to imagine that the masses of mankind were once so uneducated that they believed that their sex, race or nation was superior to another. Even though there are undoubtedly individuals who still harbor prejudices of some kind, these are regarded as mental aberrations. It is rare to find a person willing to publicly admit to a prejudice.

War and crime have almost ceased to exist. Both are approached as psychological problems and dealt with accordingly whenever possible. A few wars have occurred in recent centuries where a charismatic leader has asserted himself and misled a pueblo or a region into attacking their neighbors. In every case, the surrounding nations have combined their forces to convince the aggressor to back down.

Economy

The industrial economy is gone. It evaporated when the industrial nations poisoned themselves with tens of thousands of untested petrochemicals and genetically modified foods. As the populations in what was once called the "First World" plummeted, the corporations, financial institutions, organized religions, military-industrial complexes, and all other centers of power withered.

The violence that arose as the centers of power fought to maintain their stranglehold on humanity created intense suffering for everyone on the planet. During the collapse, desperate remnants of the dying, male-dominated order were pitted against the majority of the population who enjoyed a new enlightenment that was evolving and spreading. This new consciousness centered on life as a spiritual process supported by a healthy ecology. This struggle, between the old order and the new, has been likened to the pains of childbirth. In history, this period of time is referred to as *The Calamity*.

After The Calamity, the need to transport people and goods around the planet was vastly reduced due to several factors: the efficiency of the self-sufficient pueblos, extended families residing close to each other, efficient communication, the death of the industrial economy with its need to move raw materials and products, and the exhaustion of fossil fuels. Today, we enjoy the tranquility of our pueblo life where anything we need is only a few steps away.

There is no unemployment. Each pueblo is a busy place with many needs to be filled. During the industrial economy, tasks were moved around the world to whatever country provided the cheapest labor. Today, if a shirt is to be made, someone in the pueblo will make it. If possible, a farmer, living in the pueblo, will produce the cotton or wool, another will make the cloth. Our lives are simple compared to those of the industrial age. We measure our success in happiness, not in money.

We use donkey carts and horses for local transportation. We know how to produce aircraft and aircars, but we choose animals because we are not in a hurry to go anywhere. There is plenty of time to go a few miles at the animal's pace. For long distances, we use an elevated tube system that is extremely fast and efficient.

Before the Calamity, mankind seemed to worship technology as part of the fast-paced consumer culture. It was said, "Time is money." Technology filled people's lives with trivial activities. Now that money is of little importance, so is time. We have all the time we need for family and joy, for art and recreation.

We enjoy a global economy with a single currency, the Thaler, which has an unchanging value, set many years ago as the minimum for one hour's wage. There is no need to regulate our economy, nor is there such an occupation as an economist. There is no inflation; it went away when the concept of scarcity disappeared. Our historians joke that inflation vanished when the last known economist passed away in 2317. Perhaps that was only a coincidence.

Through global consultation, the distribution of wealth among the pueblos is gently influenced, but not controlled. If a single pueblo is found to be declining in assets, to have a negative balance of trade over an extended period of time, the region consults to see if that pueblo can produce something useful that will improve their exports. The hope is for each pueblo to have roughly equal wealth on a per capita basis. There is no mechanism to force an artificial balance.

Private ownership of small businesses is encouraged in most pueblos. Some pueblos prefer to operate as communes, either partially or totally. No effort is made by the regions, nations or planet to control the economic operations of any of the pueblos, or to force an economic system on them.

Corporations are permitted, but the stock-holders are morally and legally responsible for the actions of their corporation. Only a few national or international corporations exist; their purpose is to create equipment that is beyond the means of a single pueblo — communications or medical technology, for example. There is no financial industry as it was known during the industrial age. There is no need for huge amounts of money to accomplish the goals of the new era. There are no large banks, only a credit union in each pueblo.

The underlying assumption in our economy is that there is plenty for everyone, so no one tries to amass excessive resources or money. Everyone understands that, as their pueblo prospers, all the residents benefit. So we work for the common good, knowing that our personal lives will be, therefore, happy and mostly stress-free. We read about the cut-throat corporations of the industrial age, but it is hard for us to believe that educated humans were ever so self-destructive.

Families

Extended families tend to live close together in one pueblo. Marriages usually occur between 15 and 18 years of age and produce, on average, two or three children. The hours devoted to school or work are each less than six hours per day, so there is plenty of time for all activities, whether school, work, raising children, or helping the elderly or neighbors. Young married couples tend to live with or near their parents and grandparents so there is ample child care.

Women who choose to have a career, even one that involves advanced degrees, are able to have children without sacrificing the quality of any facet of their lives. This is made possible by the combination of adequate childcare and the few hours required for work or school.

Education

The primary focus of today's civilization is the children. The overarching criterium of every major decision is: *What is best for the next seven generations?* — a lesson learned from the indigenous cultures of every continent. Nothing else is allowed to take precedence for any reason.

Education is Montessori-like and free at all levels, including for advanced degrees. The overall goal is to produce adults who excel at problem-solving, work well as a team and improve the outcomes for everyone. The primitive educational systems of the distant past, with daily lectures by teachers to a room full of students, are non-existent. Functioning almost as librarians, our teachers help students find resources as they teach themselves and each other. Only rarely will a teacher lecture as a subject-matter expert. The older students may work from home with online links to their teachers and classmates, periodically meeting face to face as the team works to solve problems or produce cross-discipline studies. The students often work with teams in other pueblos through video conferencing.

As with everything else in the culture that has emerged over the last six hundred years, art and science dominate education. Ecological agriculture is considered the most important science, closely followed by health and wellness. During the industrial age, scientists were forced to be somewhat competitive and insular. Now, both in academia and commerce, researchers share discoveries freely so that each pueblo can progress as rapidly as possible.

Religion

Organized religion no longer exists. By the end of the industrial age, possibly due to universal education, humanity realized that the clergy of every religion were simply more groups grabbing power and resources in a delusion of scarcity. After the year 1900, the number of people attending clergy-led services rapidly declined, with each generation becoming more spiritual and less religious.

Historians have concluded that, in the first 2000 years of the Christian era, the clergy of all religions created more problems for mankind than they solved. Abolishing the clergy is seen as a major factor in reducing the number of wars since the Calamity.

Today, all the historical religions exist in personal practice, but there is no longer a need for someone to interpret scripture for a group, nor a need for separate buildings. Chapels are located within each pueblo for the use of all, regardless of belief.

Government

The government pyramid was inverted around the time that the industrial economy collapsed. Whereas national governments were previously powerful, at least to the extent that international corporations allowed them to have power, local governments are now primary. The pueblos are the only entities that can levy taxes. Regional and national governments exist only as necessary for cooperation and harmony, depending on the pueblos for donations to cover their modest costs.

The international government is led by a group of nineteen women who, at present, all happen to be grandmothers. It focuses on harmonizing the national and regional interests and has the ability to censure and punish nations who willfully disrupt the harmony. In practice that has only happened in the few cases of war. There is a world court that settles ordinary disputes.

Elections at all levels are carried out with write-in ballots. There are no political parties. Nominations and electioneering are forbidden. Actually no one wants to be elected. The First Nations peoples of North America have an ancient saying, "If a man wants to be chief, you know he isn't qualified." This belief is now pervasive throughout the planet. Persons with the most votes do the work, even if they have to be dragged, kicking and screaming, into their new office. Obviously, a majority of votes isn't required. Serving as an elected official at any level is seen as a duty, not as an opportunity for acquiring power.

Health

Health care is free for all. The cost to maintain the wellness of each pueblo is a tiny fraction of their economy. There are several reasons for the small cost of health care. Travel has been reduced drastically since the industrial economy collapsed and families chose to stay together, reducing the spread of communicable diseases. It has been over 600 years since the last vestiges of the industrial economy disappeared, so the chemical pollution caused by plastics, fossil fuels, chemical agriculture and other environmental problems, have gone away. All food is grown organically in the gardens and farms that surround each pueblo so there is very little to degrade one's natural health. In fact, we never speak of "organic" anything. Since the ecology of each farm is maintained naturally, the adjective is unnecessary.

The medical cartel, including the pharmaceutical industry, disappeared with the rest of the industrial economy. Health care now focuses on wellness, drastically reducing the need for drugs and surgery. Most healing is accomplished through food, rest, sunlight, baths of warm or cold water, and non-invasive physical modalities. All medical knowledge from all cultures has been maintained and expanded over the centuries, so doctors can treat almost anything. Compounding pharmacies within each pueblo produce any medicines required.

Architecture

The design of many pueblos is a sphere approximately 700 meters (2300 feet) in diameter with shaded gardens of fragrant flowers or herbs underneath, then concentric circles of farms extending out as far as needed to supply food and clothing. In summer, cool air from the gardens is vented up into the structure. During cold weather, the warm air in the top floors of the pueblo is pushed down to warm the lower floors.

Other pueblos are built of local materials such as stone or adobe to retain heat in the winter and cold in the summer. Individual homes are generally not used except in small villages. Various coatings for buildings have been developed to generate electricity and control light and heat. It is possible to live comfortably in most temperate and tropical areas with minimal cost.

The design life of each pueblo is at least a thousand years. This spreads the construction cost over fifty generations instead of two or three as in the temporary buildings of the industrial age.

The goal of all pueblos is to have only positive impacts on the environment. Technology has improved so that the difficulties of creating an enduring ecosystem for a pueblo have largely disappeared. The recycling of all resources, the reduced electrical demand, the improvement of communications, and the perfection of agriculture have all led to a pleasant and inexpensive lifestyle for all without negative effects on the planet.

After the industrial collapse, it was obvious that large cities like London, New York or Tokyo, by then mostly empty, were no longer of any permanent value to humans. Soon the cities were completely abandoned, then partially recycled by companies that scavenged usable materials for use in the surrounding pueblos. Windows and doors were removed from buildings to allow animals and birds to have access. Manhattan, for example, is now a bird sanctuary. Most of the buildings in the city have long since collapsed allowing trees and brush to grow on the piles of rubble. It is expected that eventually the forest will return to completely cover the former cities.

A few of the metropolises that developed late in the industrial age, like Los Angeles, have been reorganized as a cluster of pueblos by removing most of the buildings to provide agricultural space. However, this was impractical in older cities due to the density of buildings and soil pollution.

Most rivers in the world are pollution-free. Even the Hudson and East Rivers that surround Manhattan are drinkable again. Today children play in some rivers in North American that were once so polluted they could catch fire.

Art

Today, a sense of beauty informs everything we create whether a hand tool or a public park. We recognize that beauty is capable of creating joy and reducing stress, so the design of everything is influenced by its inherent beauty and its harmony with its environment. With an average work week of less than 24 hours, there is plenty of time for creativity and enjoying the artwork of others. Many people talk about "the creative life," the idea that all of life — work, recreation, entertainment, and raising children — can be part of one continuous artistic expression.

With the collapse of the cities and financial centers during the Calamity, the art world lost its Euro-centricity. There was a period, roughly between 1500 and 2500, when European art was considered collectible, some pieces fetching prices that could purchase small towns. Today art has returned to historical norms of value. It is produced in every culture, is often anonymous, and generally follows the needs and standards of the pueblo where it is produced.

There is considerable sharing of art across the internet. This has a natural influence as the styles within a pueblo slowly evolve over time.

History

We read in the histories about the struggles of the industrial age and the resulting Calamity, the battles between capital and labor, communism and democracy, between the Jews, Christians and Muslims, between white people and people of every other color. We read the words, but we can't conceive of human minds enmeshed in such dysfunction. It seems that, at that time, the concept of one human family was missing. To us, the essential oneness of mankind is as obvious as the sun. The races of mankind were, and are, like the flowers of a garden. We celebrate our differences and weep for the ignorance that once prevented mankind from seeing the unity in its own diversity.

The history of the Calamity itself was a study in human nature, both the best and the worst of it. It is generally described as a two hundred year period although the exact start and end dates are hard to identify. The processes that began in the nineteenth century to spread a spiritual influence over the planet didn't establish a firm grasp on the population until the late twenty-first century. The collapse of the old order that began in the nineteenth century was generally complete by the twenty-third century, although pockets of the old power structure continued to cause problems into the twenty-fifth.

While it could be described as a series of economic, diplomatic or physical battles between factions, most of today's historians see it as a gradual process of mankind's evolution from childish groups squabbling over resources to mature, global consultations about the best way to achieve a pleasant life for all peoples while maintaining the Earth's ecology.

Welcome to the third millennium.

The Four Noble Truths of Buddhism

This book is based, however loosely, on the *Four Noble Truths*, and the last several chapters wander along the *Eightfold Path*. I am a Bahá'í and not a Buddhist, but I believe that the Four Noble Truths are the foundation of a joyful life, and that the Eightfold path is the foundation of any life attempting to live by The Golden Rule. Hopefully this book will instill in the reader a little curiosity about this ancient wisdom.

While even a cursory explanation of the Four Noble Truths is beyond the scope of this book, here is a brief outline.

1. All human life involves suffering. We all experience illness, death, and loss.

2. The pain of this suffering comes from our grasping at ephemera. Everything physical is ephemeral, arising from something else, then transformed into yet another form. We experience pain when we are attached to a form that we don't want to change.

3. There can be a cessation of suffering. We can overcome our attachment to ephemera.

4. Suffering can be overcome by following the Eightfold Path.

The Eightfold Path

1. Right vision. It is important that we see everything clearly, as it truly is, and not how we want it to be.

2. Right intention. We must obey the Golden Rule in everything we do. Our intention must be to serve others.

3. Right speech. Rather than harm others with our words, we must always seek to benefit them.

4. Right action. When we sincerely follow through with our good intentions, we must strive to accomplish good deeds.

5. Right Livelihood. The Golden Rule must be woven into the fabric of all our business dealings. Our employees, our employer, our customers and suppliers, must all be treated so that they benefit from every transaction.

6. Right effort. We must not be lazy in our spiritual practice, nor in our physical lives. The Eight-fold Path will not be followed to the end without effort.

7. Right mindfulness. When we live only in the moment, with no anger about the past, nor fear of the future, we are able to focus on the current task with joy.

8. Right concentration. Related to mindfulness, right concentration involves both meditating with a focused mind, and acting with a focused mind.

There are a great many resources in book form and on the internet that will illuminate these important topics. Search for "Four Noble Truths."

Ron Frazer

Dr. Ron Frazer has degrees in mechanical engineering, mathematics, natural health and ninety percent of a degree in fine arts that he'll probably never finish. Apparently he doesn't know what he wants to be when he grows up.

He's lived in the US, the UK, St. Lucia and Grenada. He currently lives in a suburb of Cleveland, Ohio. On the odd occasions when he chooses reality, he lives with his naturopath wife Sandy, and a domineering Chihuahua.

Ron also plays a bad clarinet; a version of bad that makes his dog howl.

Novels

Beyond a Veil explores the spiritual growth of a woman who is dealing with her daughter's murder while struggling with a terminal illness. While it sounds like a sob-story, her spiritual growth is quite exemplary and the tone is very light-hearted.

Time Branches, the story of a woman in a coma who discovers she can move in time and space. Through a series of jumps, she takes herself further and further back in her own life as she attempts to improve the outcomes of the lives of her mother and sister. She has a bit of naughty fun in the process.

The Carib's Smile, the first book of the Jacinta Joseph trilogy, follows the adventures of a black female detective who returns to the Caribbean island where she was born, then becomes dedicated to cleaning up the corruption that is holding the country back while murdering anyone that stands in its way. The trilogy is written as both a mystery and a romantic comedy.

The Judge's wife, the second Jacinta Joseph Caribbean adventure, finds the detective joining eight other grandmothers who are intent on changing the government while she is immersed in an ocean of family problems.

The Wife's Turn is the final Jacinta Joseph Caribbean adventure where the remaining bad guys are dealt with and the economy revamped.

A Handful of Seawater, Ron's first novel, is a fictional biography of Morgan, a junk-yard dog of a boy, who starts life as the poorest of the poor on a tropical island. Read the touching story of an orphan's triumph under the Zen-like guidance of a simple fisherman who mentors him. It's a story of sex, drugs and Reggae but from the perspective of a young man's search for love, family and fulfillment.

Short Fiction

Ron's poems and short stories have been published in *Sandscript, The Blackwater Review, and The African-American Review*. His stories are based on the lives of his students and their families on the Caribbean island of Grenada where he taught math and science following the 1983 US intervention.

Non-Fiction

Staying Well: a family guide to wellness is a compilation of articles that were written as the Natural Health guru for a website. Ron has a Masters and a Ph.D. in Natural Health from Clayton College in Birmingham, AL.

Websites

Books: www.ronfrazer.com

Facebook: facebook.com/RonFrazerAuthor

Blog: ronfrazer.com/blog

Art Credits

Cover art by Efes Kitap, pixabay.com

Cover and book design by Ron Frazer

Artists mentioned in novel

Edward Povey, see www.edwardpovey.com

Eva Borowski, see www.facebook.com/eva.borowski.35

Tamara de Lempicka, see www.delempicka.org

www.ingramcontent.com/pod-product-compliance
Lightning Source LLC
Chambersburg PA
CBHW030650110726
47901CB00002B/652